Marx Hardy Abbott Defoe Machiavelli Montaigne Melville Chesterton Cooper Emerson Joyce Austen Hugo Eliot Grimm Haggard Christie Carroll Stoker Molière Wilde Maupassant Byron Schiller Garnett Engels Smith Kafka Goethe Hawthorne Einstein Fitzgerald Dostoyevsky Hall Cotton Kipling Doyle Willis Baum Henry Nietzsche Leslie Dumas Flaubert Turgenev Balzac Stockton Vatsyayana Crane Burroughs Verne Curtis Tocqueville Whitman Gogol Vinci Homer Widger Tolstoy Busch Darwin Thoreau Twain Potter Freud Zola Lawrence Scott Harte Kant Jowett Stevenson Dickens Plato London Andersen Descartes Cervantes Burton Hesse Poe Aristotle Wells Voltaire Cooke Hale James Hastings Bunner Shakespeare Richter Chambers Irving Doré da Shaw Chekhov Wodehouse Benedict Alcott Pushkin Dante Swift Newton

 tredition®

tredition was established in 2006 by Sandra Latusseck and Soenke Schulz. Based in Hamburg, Germany, tredition offers publishing solutions to authors and publishing houses, combined with world-wide distribution of printed and digital book content. tredition is uniquely positioned to enable authors and publishing houses to create books on their own terms and without conventional manu-facturing risks.

For more information please visit: www.tredition.com

TREDITION CLASSICS

This book is part of the TREDITION CLASSICS series. The creators of this series are united by passion for literature and driven by the intention of making all public domain books available in printed format again - worldwide. Most TREDITION CLASSICS titles have been out of print and off the bookstore shelves for decades. At tredition we believe that a great book never goes out of style and that its value is eternal. Several mostly non-profit literature projects provide content to tredition. To support their good work, tredition donates a portion of the proceeds from each sold copy. As a reader of a TREDITION CLASSICS book, you support our mission to save many of the amazing works of world literature from oblivion. See all available books at www.tredition.com.

Project Gutenberg

The content for this book has been graciously provided by Project Gutenberg. Project Gutenberg is a non-profit organization founded by Michael Hart in 1971 at the University of Illinois. The mission of Project Gutenberg is simple: To encourage the creation and distribu-tion of eBooks. Project Gutenberg is the first and largest collection of public domain eBooks.

A Vanished Hand

Sarah Doudney

Imprint

This book is part of TREDITION CLASSICS

Author: Sarah Doudney
Cover design: Buchgut, Berlin – Germany

Publisher: tredition GmbH, Hamburg - Germany
ISBN: 978-3-8472-1564-6

www.tredition.com
www.tredition.de

A
VANISHED
HAND
NISBET

A VANISHED HAND

BY SARAH DOUDNEY

AUTHOR OF "WHERE THE DEW FALLS IN LONDON,"
ETC. ETC.

WITH ILLUSTRATIONS

London
JAMES NISBET & CO., LIMITED
21 BERNERS STREET

Printed by Ballantyne, Hanson & Co.
At the Ballantyne Press

SHE PUT THE ROLL OF PAPER INTO HIS HAND

CONTENTS

LIST OF ILLUSTRATIONS

A VANISHED HAND

CHAPTER I

IN A BACK ROOM

> "For one shall grasp, and one resign,
> One drink life's rue, and one its wine,
> And God shall make the balance good."

> —Whittier.

Elsie Kilner had a battle to fight, and it must be fought after her own fashion. It was the kind of battle which is fought every day and every hour; but the battlefield is always a silent place, and there is neither broken weapon nor crimson stain to tell us where the strife has been.

Elsie's battle was fought in a back room in All Saints' Street on an afternoon in March. It was not a gloomy room; although the window looked out upon walls and roofs and chimneys, she had a good clear view of the sky. Some pigeons occupied a little house outside one of the neighbouring windows, and there was a roof covered with red tiles on which they loved to strut and plume their feathers in the sunshine.

To a woman country-born the sight of pigeons and red tiles called up visions of an old home. The memories which came to Elsie in her London room were as fresh and sweet as the breath of early spring flowers.

She could see again the red manor-house among the Sussex hills, and the old green garden which winter could never quite despoil. The cherry-tree spread its boughs close to her window, and seemed to fill the room with the delicate dewy light of its blossoms; the winds came blowing in, sweet and chill, from thymy common and "sheep-trimmed down."

Perhaps she had never seen her home so plainly with her bodily eyes as she saw it now in imagination. Our everyday blessings are too common to be looked at in their true light; but when time and change have put them far away from us we see them in all their beauty.

"It makes me feel desperate," she said half aloud to herself.

She had a dark, delicate face, as changeful as an April sky. It was not a happy face; the dark eyes were restless, the soft lips often quivered. And yet, in spite of sorrow and unrest, and the experiences of nearly nine-and-twenty years, there was an extraordinary freshness, almost girlishness, in her appearance, which did not suffer even from the close proximity of younger women. The mourning dress, fitting closely to her graceful figure, told its own story of recent loss.

In that old manor-house among the Sussex hills her bright youth had been calmly spent. Then came her mother's death, and changes began in the home-life. Her father was growing weak in mind and body. Elsie was the only daughter, and the household cares and anxieties pressed heavily on her heart and brain. When Robert, her brother, suggested, with all possible kindliness, that it would be well if he came with his wife to the Manor and shared her labours, she welcomed the proposal gladly.

So Robert and Bertha arrived, bringing with them their little girl and her governess; and the old peace fled away for ever.

For two miserable years Elsie lived on in that altered home, and saw everything that she had loved sliding gradually out of her hold. Robert introduced many new plans, all for his father's comfort, as he continually declared. Bertha took charge of the household, and the simple habits of the past were given up. Old servants were pronounced incompetent and dismissed; and when Elsie protested against these changes, her brother and his wife dropped the mask of civility.

There is no need to go over all the details of the wretched story. Old Mr. Kilner, growing more feeble every day, suffered himself to be guided entirely by Robert and Bertha, and Elsie soon found that his heart was turned away from her. Then came the end. The will was read, and everything was left to Robert Kilner.

"But Elsie cannot say that she is not provided for," said Bertha to her friends. "Her godmother — old Mrs. Hardie, you know — left her a hundred and fifty a year. Quite a fortune, is it not?"

Turned out of the old home, Elsie had come straight to London, and had sought shelter at a boarding-school where a friend of hers was a teacher. Then, after a careful search of six months, a friend had directed her to this quiet house, and she had gratefully settled here. She welcomed solitude as one who has so many things to think over, that it is indispensable.

There was a letter grasped tightly in her hand, as she stood looking out of the window. It had come from the rector's wife, who had been her mother's friend in happy days gone by. The old lady had written to say that there were wild doings at the Manor, and the country-side was ringing with tales of Robert's extravagance and dissipation. The Kilners had never been wealthy; there was just enough to keep up the old house in quiet comfort, and that was all.

"Robert will soon come to an end of everything," wrote the clergyman's wife with the frankness of long friendship. "We have heard that he was deeply involved before he came to live at the Manor. Bertha is beginning to look sad and worn and crestfallen. People have looked coldly on her since you went away, and if she ever had any influence over her husband, she has lost it now. The air is full of unwholesome rumours. I am glad that you are no longer here, my dear child."

The letter had given Elsie a cruel pleasure — a pleasure which was so hideous that her better self could not endure the sight of it. It was only the darker side of her nature which could entertain this hateful joy for a moment. And so the battle began in her heart on that sunny March afternoon.

There were certain outer influences which seemed to act upon that inward strife. The sky helped her with glimpses of holy blue and faint hints of the coming spring. Even the spire of a church helped her, although it could only point a very little way up into the far heaven. She stood quite still, wrestling silently with that fierce temptation to rejoice over her enemy's downfall.

All Bertha's insulting speeches and unkind actions came back into her mind. It might be impossible to love her, but it was—it must be—possible to be sorry for her blighted life and darkened home. Elsie called up a vision of the dressy, well-to-do Bertha, who had always put herself into a front place, and wondered how she could play the part of a neglected wife, looked down upon by her neighbours and forgotten by the world?

The thought of the crushed woman, who had so little in her interior world to help her, was not without effect. Pity triumphed. Elsie's dark eyes were suddenly dimmed with tears; she was grieved for Bertha and ashamed of herself. The fight was over, and a voice within her seemed to say that it would never have to be so fiercely fought again.

She drew a deep breath of relief as she turned away from the window, putting the letter into her pocket. The tea-tray, with its solitary cup and saucer, was waiting on the table, and Elsie poured out tea, congratulating herself that she was alone. She was not an unsociable woman; but the boarding-school, with all its noisy, merry occupants, had set her longing for solitude. She had felt far too weary and dispirited to enter into the fun and prattle of the girls.

While she drank her tea she glanced round the little room, surveying the decorations which had kept her busy for a day or two. Some relics of her old home-life were gathered here—a quaint oval looking-glass, some bits of ancient china, some photographs, and a goodly number of books. Her little clock ticked cheerfully on the mantelpiece, one or two richly-coloured fans and screens brightened the walls; there was a faint scent of sandal-wood in the air. She had not yet unlocked the handsome desk which stood on a table in the corner, and it occurred to her that she would answer some of her neglected letters that very evening.

Going to the desk, and opening it, she noticed for the first time the table on which it had been placed. It stood in the darkest part of the room, and she had not observed its old-fashioned claw feet and the curiously-wrought brass handles of its drawer. It was not a sham drawer, but a real one, which opened easily with a gentle pull, and appeared at first sight to be quite empty.

"It is large enough to hold a good many of my treasures," thought Elsie, putting in her hand. "And here are some old papers, quite at the back! I will take them out to make room for other things."

The papers were not old nor discoloured by time, although the dust had settled upon them pretty thickly. They looked like pages torn out of a diary, and were covered with writing which struck Elsie with a sense of familiarity. This handwriting, firm, black, legible, was like her own.

"How interesting!" she said to herself. "I have always flattered myself that mine was an uncommon hand. But somebody—a woman evidently—has stolen my e's and b's and g's and y's. I should like to know a little more about her."

She forgot all about the open desk and unanswered letters, and sat down on the edge of the sofa near the window with the papers on her lap. The shadow had vanished from the delicate expressive face; the dark eyes had brightened. Elsie had the happy temperament which is charmed with every little bit of novelty that it can find. She loved, as she had often said, to investigate things, and always caught eagerly at the slightest clue which might lead to a delightful labyrinth of mystery.

The manuscript began abruptly. The first words on which Elsie's glance rested were these: "If I could only be sure that some one would be kind to little Jamie!"

This sentence was written at the top of the first page, and then came a vacant space. Lower down, in the middle of the leaf, the writer had gone on: "What a new life came to me all at once when I met Harold for the first time! The path was so flowery and bright that I had no fear of the turnings of the way. It seemed the most natural thing in the world that we should meet, and walk on together all our lives. No, we did not meet; he overtook me as I was sauntering along, and looked into my face with that look which a man gives the woman who is to belong to him for ever and ever."

Elsie paused in her reading and lifted her gaze thoughtfully to the evening sky. Her face had changed again; the expression of eyes and mouth was wistful and tender.

"No man has ever loved me in that fashion," she mused. "I've had lovers, but I was never meant for them nor they for me. I wonder why this unknown woman had the joy of finding her spirit-mate when such a joy has been denied to me? Are they married? Where is she now? I wish I knew her."

No one who had seen Elsie at that moment would have doubted that she had had lovers. She was very pretty to-day; prettier at twenty-eight than she had been in the days of girlhood. Some new feeling of peace was creeping into her heart and hushing all its turmoil into a sweet rest. Some new interest was beginning to stir in her life; much was quieted within her, and much was wakening. She felt as if she had roused after an uneasy sleep and tasted the first freshness of a fair morning.

She sat a little while in silence, thinking about the unknown writer and her Harold. Although she had read only a few lines, she felt drawn towards this woman whom she had never seen. It would have been good to have had her for a friend.

Where was she now? Living somewhere with Harold, perhaps far away in the country. Elsie could fancy the pair coming homeward through ferny lanes in the first shade of the twilight. She pictured the woman, dark-eyed and dark-haired, like herself, and the man tall and fair, with a grave yet gentle face. They had a great deal to say to each other, as those who are one in spirit often have. They answered each other's thoughts; there was the fulness of a calm content in every tone.

And then she turned again to the manuscript.

CHAPTER II

WHAT WAS WRITTEN

> "And Love lives on, and hath a power to bless,
> When they who loved are hidden in the grave."

—Lowell.

"Every one said that it was a hopeless thing to get engaged to a poor curate," the writer went on, "and I was only a poor teacher, so the folly was not all on one side. We were wonderfully happy in our folly, so happy that we were full of pity for Mr. Worldly Wiseman when he happened to cross our path with his contemptuous smile. Even Harold's sister Ellen, with her cold blue eyes, had no power to chill us in those days. Frigid as Ellen was, I liked her better than James, her husband, who always pretended to be fond of me. He was a man of the 'good fellow' type—burly, and loud of voice. But Jamie, dear little lad, bore no resemblance to his father at all, and was only like his mother in her best moods. Oh, poor little Jamie!

"I am not writing a novel; I am only telling of things that really came to pass.

"We had been engaged nearly twelve months, when an old man died and left Harold £2000. I do not expect any one to understand the gladness which that money gave us. It is enough to say that I began to prepare my wedding clothes, and Harold went hunting for suitable lodgings in all his spare moments. The clothes were finished, and the lodgings found, when a terrible thing happened.

"James had always known all about Harold's affairs. He knew that our money was lying at the bank, waiting till a good investment was decided upon. He pretended to have found a safe investment, and he got the money into his own hands and absconded.

"Ellen confessed afterwards that she had known of her husband's difficulties for many months. She feigned ignorance of his whereabouts, but I always believed that she knew more than she told.

"As I said just now, I am not writing a novel; I am telling things in the plainest way, and in the fewest words. Most people, I daresay, would have survived the loss of £2000, but our hope was taken from us with the money. Harold was not strong. He was the kind of man who needs a wife's love and care, and the thought of our prolonged separation was more than he could endure. He went about his parish work as usual; no one missed a kind word because his heart ached, no good deed was left undone because his hands were tired. And yet, O Harold, how hard it was for you to labour in those days!

"He carried his cross manfully, although he staggered sometimes under its weight. And he bore his great wrong with that mighty patience which he had learnt from his Master.

"It was in the early spring that a sickness broke out among the poorest of his flock, and Harold had but little leisure. One night he was summoned from his bed to visit a dying man who prayed that he would come. And that night, when the bitter east wind smote him and the rain beat upon him, he heard the Master's call to rest.

"Do not think that I am an unhappy woman. I went down with him to the very brink of the river—that river which has been a terror unto many, but had no gloom for him. In those last moments I believe he knew that we should not be parted long; I see now that he had that swift glimpse into the future which is sometimes granted to a departing saint. How can I be unhappy when I am so sure that he is watching for me?

"Ellen sent for me to come to her. She says she has got a death-blow. James has written, telling her that she must never expect to see him again. He has deserted her for some one else, leaving her to struggle on here in poverty with her child. She has now confessed that she knew that James meant to get possession of Harold's money; she was in his confidence from the beginning.

"'We wanted to prevent your marriage with Harold if we could,' she said. 'We never liked you, Meta; but you are avenged. I sent for you to tell you that you are avenged on me.'

"Just for a moment my heart cried out that this was as it should be. Within me there was a struggle, brief and strong. But how could my better nature fail to triumph, helped as I was by Harold's loving influence? Oh, my love in heaven, I will not be conquered by evil; you are on my side—you, and the angels of God!

"It is bitter weather. I sit, up at night to mend and make Jamie's clothes, while he sleeps soundly in my bed. Dear little fellow; it does me good to see his cheeks so rosy and round, and his curly golden head half-buried in the pillow. 'If thine enemy hunger, feed him,' said the Master. It might be hard to feed mine enemy, but it is a labour of love to feed mine enemy's child.

"If I am called away, who will take care of Jamie? My landlady, Mrs. Penn, is a good woman, but one can hardly expect her to take up the burden of a little boy. And yet I think Jamie would be more of a blessing than a burden. He has the sweetest ways I ever knew, and there is a look of Harold in his blue eyes. How the wind howls to-night!

"It is a melancholy November.

"It was a curious thing that I should have a fainting fit in the street. Poor Jamie would not let my hand go when they carried me into a shop. When I came to myself I saw his dear, frightened little face looking up at me. He is not yet four years old—and I am getting weaker and weaker.

"I will write to Harold's old college friend if I can find out his address. It must be somewhere among Harold's papers. Arnold Wayne—ah, I wonder if Arnold Wayne will be good to the boy?

"Last night I had a dream of Christmas. Harold came to me in my dream, and said that I should hear the angels sing on Christmas day. I woke up to find the frosty moonlight shining into the room, and Jamie, half awake, complaining of the cold. I folded him closely in my arms, and we both fell asleep.

"I am very feeble to-day. I must not try to go out of doors. There is a little money in hand. Jamie looks at me and kisses me. Oh, Jamie!"

That was all. The handwriting, so firm at first, was straggling and faint at the close. Twilight was creeping fast into the little back room; the fire was getting low, and Elsie shivered in the chillness.

She knew now that this woman, whom she had almost envied, had passed away from earth. They were together—Harold and Meta—in the home of souls, where love finds its full satisfaction and rest.

Perhaps Elsie's vision of the pair was not as unreal as it might have been supposed to be. The thought came to her, as she sat musing in the twilight, that wherever there was a home there must surely be homeliness. The hope of a home, denied to them on earth, was realised in the eternal life—that life which has no need of marriage because the spiritual union is complete without the earthly tie.

She folded up the manuscript carefully and reverently, and put it back into the drawer of the table. But in doing this she did not put it out of her mind. Where was Jamie now? It seemed to her, that evening, as if the vanished hand of the writer were beckoning her onward to begin the search for the boy.

Meta had been wronged, and had suffered, oh, how deeply! Meta had fought the good fight and had won the victory. And to Elsie, in her loneliness, there came a great longing to take up the love-task which Meta had been suddenly called to resign, and care for Jamie as the dead woman had cared for him.

But how was she to begin her search for the child? She knew him only as Jamie. By some curious oversight Meta had not given any of the surnames of those whose story she had written. There were but two surnames mentioned in the manuscript, Penn and Wayne.

Mrs. Penn was a landlady; Arnold Wayne had been the college friend of Harold.

Elsie moved quietly about her room, busy with many thoughts as she lighted the lamp and shut out the evening sky. It was a beautiful sky, with soft rose tints touching the grey of the gloaming, and a star gleamed faintly above the tall spire. She gave a wistful look at that star before she drew down the window-blind.

CHAPTER III

TAKING COUNSEL

> "But round me, like a silver bell
> Rung down the listening sky to tell
> Of holy help, a sweet voice fell."

> —Whittier.

"I shall consult Miss Saxon," said Elsie to herself. Sunshine was streaming in through the Venetian shutters of her bedroom, and the street was waking up to its busy morning life. The light rested in soft yellow bars upon the wall, and lit up the pretty frilled toilet-cover which Miss Saxon's hands had made. To those hands belonged that good gift of womanly skill which is a blessing to any household. Already Elsie had learnt to rely upon their owner, and believe in her sagacity. If any one could help her in her perplexity, it was surely Miss Saxon.

A spirit of peace seemed to brood over her little sitting-room when she sat down to breakfast. Perhaps the scene of a spiritual victory is destined, ever afterwards, to know an atmosphere of repose.

Out of doors there was the clear blue of the spring sky, the whiteness of snowy clouds floating out of the reach of the smoke, the cheerful light warming the red tiles whereon the pigeons were taking their morning exercise. Altogether the world seemed to wear an encouraging aspect that day.

Miss Saxon had that gentleness of expression and manner which is often sweetest when youth has fled. When Elsie, with her black dress and sad face, had come to the house, she was cheered by a hundred little tokens of thoughtful kindness. The good fairy who had made the frilled toilet-cover was always at work, and her goodwill was manifested in pretty little flounces and furbelows, which gave a sort of old-fashioned grace to the rooms.

A little later Elsie was pouring out the story of her discovery of the manuscript, and Miss Saxon was listening in her quiet fashion. But her first words gave Elsie a chill of disappointment.

"At present I don't see how I can help you, Miss Kilner," she said. "That old table came into the house a few days before you arrived. I happened to see it outside a broker's shop, and thought it would be the very thing I wanted to fill up that corner."

"And the shop — is it near here?" Elsie asked anxiously.

"Very near; but I don't know much about the shopkeepers. The man seemed rather rough, but the woman was decent and civil. We will go and make inquiries."

"I thought that Meta had lived here," Elsie said in a disappointed voice.

"No. Your rooms were occupied for six years by a single gentleman. He had something to do in the City, and seemed to be a confirmed bachelor. But he married at last, and the rooms were vacant till you came to them."

"If Meta had ever lived in this street you would have known something about her, would you not?" Elsie asked.

"I might have known. We have lived here for many years, and have seen many changes. But there is no reason to suppose that she was ever here. We have first to learn where the table came from before we can get any clue that can be followed."

So those two, Miss Saxon and her eager lodger, went out together while the morning was still fresh and bright.

Looking back on that morning afterwards, Elsie remembered that everybody seemed to be seeking something. People were hastening along; women were going to the churches where there were daily services; sisters, in their white caps and black draperies, marshalled a troop of little girls in red cloaks, and seemed to have a world of business on their hands; men stepped on briskly with a preoccupied air. In all there was the great expectant human nature ever urging onward. In all there was the universal life-quest. Many, if they had known what manner of quest it was which had called Elsie forth, would have laughed her to scorn; others would have wondered; some might have wished her God-speed.

Leaving the two churches behind, Miss Saxon led the way into another street in which a perpetual market was held. Here there were hungry faces, sottish faces, sickly faces, and an endless pushing and jostling around the costermongers' barrows. It was a touching thing to see the poor bargaining for flowers—ay, and a hopeful thing, too, to those who can interpret signs aright.

They came at length to an old horse-hair sofa, an iron bedstead, a bath, and two or three hearth-rugs; and behind these articles there was a narrow door, which Elsie entered with some reluctance.

If you are fastidious or superstitious, a broker's shop in a low neighbourhood is hardly the place that you will choose to visit. One does not know what unwholesome associations may be clinging to the chairs and carpets and pillows which hem you in on every side; or one naturally recalls wild stories of haunted banjoes and tambourines, and tables which are said to slide about in an uncanny fashion of their own accord.

Elsie was no weaker-minded than most women, but it must be confessed that she followed her guide through that dark doorway after a moment's hesitation.

There was, however, nothing weird about the aspect of the woman who came forward, with a baby in her arms, to greet Miss Saxon. She was still young and pretty, with that delicate London prettiness which meets one in these crowded thoroughfares at every turn. The baby had a shawl drawn over its bald head, and peered out from its shelter with eyes just beginning to observe the sundry and manifold changes of its little world.

"It is rather more than a fortnight ago since I bought a table here," Miss Saxon began. "It was a very old-fashioned table with brass handles and claw feet. Do you remember it?"

"Yes, ma'am, I do," replied the woman, after a moment's consideration.

"Here is a lady who wishes to know where that table came from. She fancies it belonged to some one in whom she takes an interest," continued Miss Saxon in her quiet voice. "We have come to know if you can tell us anything about it?"

Elsie's heart throbbed fast in the pause that followed. The baby looked at her and gave a faint chuckle, as if it triumphed in the thought that even grown-up people cannot find out all the puzzles of life.

"It came from a house in Dashwood Street," the woman said at last. "They had a regular turn-out of old furniture, and my husband bought a good many things. I'll go and ask him the number of the house."

She disappeared into a gloomy region at the back of the shop, and was lost to sight for a minute or two.

"He says 'twas 132," she said, emerging from the gloom, baby and all.

"We're very much obliged to you," returned Miss Saxon.

"Not at all, ma'am. Glad to have been of use to you."

Elsie came away gaily from the broker's door, in the belief that she was going to walk straight to the goal. But Miss Saxon was less sanguine. Moreover, she had no great faith in the manuscript, and seemed disposed to think that it was written by some one who wanted to make a story.

"It might have been intended for a magazine," she suggested, "and the writer broke off short. We have no proof at all that Meta was a real person."

"I own I have no proof," Elsie admitted frankly. "But I have a feeling that I must seek out Jamie."

"But perhaps Meta is living and taking care of him still, Miss Kilner. People don't always die when they think their end is near. As a matter of fact, the more they think they are going the longer they stay."

"I know she is dead—I feel it," rejoined Elsie, with unshaken conviction. "I am guided by intuition. It seems like a blind leap into the dark, but I must search for Jamie."

Miss Saxon looked kindly into the dark eyes which met hers with such an earnest gaze.

"Something may come of it," she said after a pause. "Well, Miss Kilner, I promised to help you, and I will."

Elsie clasped her hands suddenly. "I can't do without your help," she cried. "Dear Miss Saxon, you are one of the born helpers—some are born hinderers, you know. Oh, how glad I am that I am come to you!"

"I'm glad too," Miss Saxon answered, with quiet warmth. And then they walked away together in silence, across Portland Place and on to Dashwood Street.

No. 132 was a house which looked as if it could never have contained anything so old-fashioned as Elsie's table. It had been smartened up till it looked more like a doll's house than a human habitation. In the windows there were yellow muslin curtains tied with pink sashes, and amber flower-pots holding sham plants of the most verdant hue. The maid who opened the door exactly matched the house. She was like a cheap doll, very smart, very pert, and capped and aproned in the latest style.

In answer to Miss Saxon's question she gave a curt reply.

"No; nobody of the name of Penn had ever lived in that house. Mrs. Dodge was the mistress. She didn't know anything about the name of Penn. Mrs. Dodge took the house about two months ago."

"Please take my card to Mrs. Dodge," said Elsie, in a manner which instantly took effect.

They were invited to walk into a hall which smelt of new oil-cloth, and were solemnly ushered into the room with the green linen plants and yellow blinds. Presently Mrs. Dodge, dressed in harmony with her house, came in with a rustle and a flourish. She was a big woman, with hair so yellow and cheeks so rosy, that she seemed the very person to preside over this gaily-coloured establishment.

At a sign from Miss Saxon, Elsie took the questioning into her own hands. She described the table to begin with.

Mrs. Dodge was bland and civil. She had taken the house of her aunt, an old lady who was getting too infirm to attend to lodgers. It was filled from top to bottom with the most hideous old things, and she had put them all into the broker's hands. She fancied she remembered the table, but could not be certain; there were a good many queer old tables.

No; she had never heard the name of Penn. But she had a young sister who knew all her aunt's friends better than she did. She should be called.

The sister was called, and proved to be a young and smiling copy of Mrs. Dodge. She remembered that she had once seen Mrs. Penn, about two years ago. Mrs. Penn was a small spare woman about fifty. Yes; Mrs. Penn had let lodgings somewhere — she didn't know where — and her aunt had bought some of her furniture. There was an old table with claw-feet, among other things.

"Was the aunt living now?" Elsie asked.

"Oh, yes; she was living at Winchfield," the girl answered. But she was deaf and rather cross, and it was a hard matter to make her understand anything. "Mrs. Tryon, Stone Cottage, Winchfield, near the railway station."

Elsie wrote the address in her note-book, and left Dashwood Street with hope renewed.

"We are getting nearer to the goal," she said brightly. "You see now that Mrs. Penn is a real person."

"And if Mrs. Penn is real, then Meta and Harold and Jamie are real also," Miss Saxon replied. "Yes, I think you have proved that they are not mere phantoms."

"And that is proving a good deal in a world which is fall of uncertainties," Elsie cried. "Don't laugh at me, Miss Saxon; I hear a voice calling me to go on! You cannot hear it, I know, but you must trust to my ears."

"I will trust you," Miss Saxon answered, with an admiring glance at the slight erect figure by her side. Elsie was a little above middle height, and she walked with the step of a woman who has been accustomed to an out-of-door life, as naturally graceful as the swaying of the grasses on a hillside.

All Saints' Street was still warm with the morning sunshine when they came back to their door, and Elsie ran upstairs to her rooms with a light step. Difficulties and trials were to come, but she had made a beginning.

CHAPTER IV

MRS. TRYON

> "Just when I seemed about to learn!
> Where is the thread now? Off again!
> The old trick! Only I discern —

Infinite passion and the pain
Of finite hearts that yearn."

— Browning.

"A Letter will not do," said Elsie to her counsellor. "If Mrs. Tryon is a cross person she won't take the trouble to answer a letter. So I shall go to Winchfield."

"Well, it isn't a long journey," Miss Saxon replied, "and the weather is lovely. A glimpse of the country won't do you any harm."

The glimpse of the country did not do any harm, but it awakened a host of sleeping memories.

When she got out of the train at the quiet station there was the familiar breath of wallflowers in the air. It was a flower which her old father had loved, and she seemed to see him walking along the garden paths, gathering a nosegay for his wife in the early morning. Birds were singing the old blithe songs which they had sung in her childhood; there was a flutter of many wings among the boughs, which as yet were unclothed with green. Country voices came ringing across the fields and over the hedges; country faces, stolid and rosy, met her as she turned slowly into the sunny road leading to the village.

It was not difficult to find Stone Cottage, and, wonderful to relate, it was really built of unadorned grey stone, not of brick. Time had done much to soften the severe aspect of this sturdy habitation; creepers clung to the grey walls—not wholly hiding them, but breaking up the dull uniformity of neutral tint. In the little garden there was such a brave show of jonquils and daffodils that it looked like a golden paradise.

Mrs. Tryon was sitting by the fire in a little room which opened into the kitchen. She was deaf and her sight was dim, but it pleased her to believe that she still kept ears and eyes open to her servant's delinquencies. Years of letting lodgings had developed all the suspicious instincts of her nature; the domestic servant, she argued, was the same all the world over, and always to be regarded with unmitigated distrust. To the last day of her life, Mrs. Tryon would look upon the maid-of-all-work as her natural foe.

The fire was bright; scarlet geraniums made a red glow in flower-pots on the window-sill; a gay china mug, filled with daffodils, stood in the middle of the table; it was no wonder that Elsie received an impression of warmth and gaudy colours when she entered the room. The old woman with the soured face and white hair was the only chilly thing to be seen.

"I don't want Mrs. Dodge to be sending people here," she said, after hearing Elsie's explanation of her visit. "A light-minded, rollicking woman is my niece Dodge. She'll never make that house pay its expenses—never!"

"You knew Mrs. Penn, I think?" began Elsie, anxious to turn the conversation away from the Dodge subject.

"I used to know her when I was in London."

"Where is she now?" Elsie asked anxiously.

"That I can't tell you. She was never a great friend of mine. I was too busy to make friends. She had part of a house in Soho Square. Some people in business had the first floor. But I think she's gone."

"Did you ever hear her speak of a lady called Meta?" inquired Elsie, in a voice that slightly trembled.

"Meta? No; I've never heard the name. Who was she? An actress, I suppose?"

"Oh, no!" replied Elsie hastily. "She was some one who lived with Mrs. Penn."

"Ah, there was a young lady who occupied one room at the top of the house, and did pictures for the papers and cheap magazines. I never saw her, but Mrs. Penn spoke of her once or twice, and seemed mightily concerned when she died."

"Then Mrs. Penn spoke to you of her death?" Elsie said breathlessly.

"Yes; she was a weak-minded woman, Mrs. Penn was, and allowed herself to be upset by trifles. She said that Miss Somebody was dead—I never could remember names; the name don't matter—and she had called to ask if I wanted any furniture. I said I'd take a couple of small tables and an arm-chair if she'd let me have 'em cheap. I knew she'd got some good, substantial old things."

"And had this furniture been in the young lady's room?" asked Elsie.

"Some of it had, I suppose. She told me that she didn't mean to let the room again; she was going to sleep in it herself," she said, "because it was large and light."

There was a brief pause. The clatter of teacups in the kitchen warned Elsie that she had trespassed on the old woman's patience long enough. A tabby cat, which had been asleep by the fire, got up, stretched itself, and came purring round its mistress's chair.

"Pussy knows it's tea-time," said Mrs. Tryon, bending down to stroke the creature.

Elsie rose to depart.

"One word more," she said, stooping to bring her lips closer to the deaf ear.

Mrs. Tryon glanced up impatiently.

"I never could stand many questions," she muttered.

"Only one more. Did Mrs. Penn ever mention a little boy who lived with the poor young lady?"

"Never," the old woman answered. "And now that's the end of it all, I hope. I shall let my niece, Dodge, know what I think of her for sending folks to trouble me in my old age. Mrs. Penn was no great friend of mine. I never went inside her door more than twice, and I never set eyes on the artist-lady, living or dead. As to the number of her house, it's gone clean out of my mind!"

The interview was ended; and as Elsie went forth again into the afternoon sunshine she felt a chill of disappointment.

She had learnt definitely that Meta had lived and died in Mrs. Penn's house, that the house was in Soho Square, and that was all. There was nothing about Jamie; and it was Jamie, not Meta, who was the object of her search.

The air was fresh and sweet. A little puff of wind blew the scent of hyacinths into her face. A pretty child smiled at her over a cottage gate, its golden curls tossed by the breeze.

Again she thought of Jamie, picturing the rosy face and golden curls, like those which Meta had described. If she could find the boy, she felt, with a sudden heart-throb, that she must hold him fast. No woman's life is complete without a child's presence in it. There are a hundred ways of filling up the void, but only one natural way. Elsie Kilner was nearly nine-and-twenty, and she was hungering, half unconsciously, after a child's love.

She caught a delicious glimpse of woods, just touched with that first shade of green which no artist has ever truthfully rendered. Men can paint summer and autumn, but the promise of the seasons escapes them; it is too subtle for brush or pencil. You may as well try to paint a perfume or a sigh.

And yet, as Elsie thought, walking onward, there is something in these beginnings which is sadder even than the summer's ending. Birth is the herald of decay and death, but decay and death are the sure forerunners of new life.

The afternoon was deepening into evening when she found herself again in All Saints' Street, and Miss Saxon's pleasant face greeted her at the door.

"Any news, Miss Kilner?" was the first question.

"No news of Jamie," Elsie answered sadly. "But I must try to find Mrs. Penn's house in Soho Square."

"Does she live there now?" Miss Saxon asked.

"Mrs. Tryon thinks not. She couldn't remember the number."

"That does not matter," said Miss Saxon cheerfully. "The square is not very large; it will only take a little while to go from door to door."

The last light of the day was shining into Elsie's sitting-room when she went upstairs, and it was a light which seemed to flow in like a golden wave from some unseen ocean of peace.

Had she come into this quiet house to be guided, by a vanished hand, along a path which she knew not? All she was sure of was the influence which had turned her feet out of the old road, so thickly set with thorns. Surely it was a kindly power which had led her away from the contemplation of her own grief and wrongs, and had given her a quest!

Something to do, something to seek and to hope for—this is the greatest blessing which can be conferred on a lonely life.

Elsie lighted her lamp, and wrote a long, cheery letter to the rector's wife in the Sussex village; but not one word did she say about the search for Jamie.

CHAPTER V

MRS. BEATON

> "Guided thus, O friend of mine,
> Let us walk our little way;
> Knowing by each beckoning sign
> That we are not quite astray."
>
> —Whittier.

It was difficult for Elsie, entering Soho Square for the first time, to realise that it had been one of the most fashionable parts of London till far into the last century. That touch of distinction which still lingers about some of the former haunts of greatness has entirely deserted this old square, and it requires an effort to picture the state of the four ambassadors and the pomp of the nobility who once made it their home. But the garden lacks not that charm of shadowy trees which so often lends a grace to the nooks and corners of the great city, and it is green enough to rest the eyes that are weary with watching the endless march of life.

Elsie made inquiries at a shop in Charles Street, and was fortunate enough to light upon a tradesman who knew something of Mrs. Penn. She had left the neighbourhood, he believed, but he could tell the number of the house she had occupied. It was close by, on the left hand as you entered the square.

As Mrs. Tryon had said, the ground-floor was given up to business, but the upper floors were still let to lodgers. A quiet-looking young widow appeared in answer to Elsie's summons. "No, ma'am, I didn't know Mrs. Penn," she said civilly. "She gave up this house nearly two years ago, and I've only been here six months. It was my sister who took the house after Mrs. Penn."

"Then there is no hope of getting the information I want," sighed Elsie; "unless any of Mrs. Penn's lodgers are here still."

"No, ma'am," said the widow again; "they are all new-comers. I am sorry that I can't help you."

There was a pause; Elsie was hesitating before she made a request. "There is a room at the top of the house which I should like to see," she said with an effort.

"There are three rooms at the very top," the landlady answered. "Two are small, but the front room is a good size."

"It is the largest room which I want to see," Elsie said.

The widow considered for a moment. "It's let to a gentleman who teaches languages and translates foreign books into English," she remarked at last. "He's out now, I think. Will you follow me, ma'am?"

Elsie's heart beat faster. As she ascended flight after flight of stairs she told herself that there was nothing to be learnt by going into the room which Meta had occupied, and yet she had a longing to be there.

They gained the top at last, and as they crossed the threshold of the chamber a dash of rain beat suddenly against the windows. Elsie's hands were clasped together tightly under her cloak. She was thinking of those winter nights when Meta lay here shivering with Jamie by her side; she thought of the lonely hours, when the house was still, and the weary worker had sat up to mend the little garments which should keep the cold from the boy. It was such a meagre tale which Meta had told. But Elsie, with her woman's heart and quick intelligence, could fill in all the details.

The sunshine followed the rain. While she stood musing in silence a light broke through the clouds and shone right into the room. That light brought with it a sudden feeling of Sabbath calm and peace. The wonderful inner consciousness (which seems to be wanting in some natures) received a message of quietness and comfort, and Elsie knew, with quiet certainty, that Meta's sufferings were not worthy to be compared with the bright rest which she had won.

They only stayed for a few minutes upstairs, and then went down in silence. As Elsie, a little tired now, was passing out into the square again the widow suddenly recalled her. "There's an old lady in Wardour Street who used to know Mrs. Penn," she said; "a Mrs. Beaton. She keeps her son's house. You'd find her at No. 127."

In a moment Elsie's weariness was forgotten. The sun was shining; it was still early in the afternoon; her time was all her own. She thanked the civil widow, and turned her steps at once towards Wardour Street.

If she had not been so deeply absorbed in her purpose she must have paused, arrested by the quaint things which were displayed in Beaton's window. It was not, perhaps, more fascinating than other windows in that wonderful street, but it had a great store of delicate ivory carvings and lovely mosaics. Yet Elsie merely gave a passing glance at these treasures, and, passing swiftly into the dim interior of the shop, asked if she could see Mrs. Beaton.

A sallow man, who was young without youthfulness, looked at her with an expression of surprise. She began to explain the object of her visit. "I am in search of a Mrs. Penn," she said frankly. "I have been to the house in Soho Square which she used to occupy, and I was directed here."

"We knew Mrs. Penn," the man answered; "but my mother seldom sees people. However, I'll ask if she can give you any information."

He disappeared, and a pale-faced lad stepped quickly into his place behind the counter. After waiting for a few moments Elsie heard a door close, and he came back. "My mother hasn't heard from Mrs. Penn since she left Soho Square," he said. "She cannot tell you anything about her."

An exclamation of disappointment broke from Elsie's lips; she moved impatiently, turning her face towards the door. The man looked at her keenly, with dark eyes shining through his spectacles.

"If you knew Mrs. Penn," she began, with a quiver of distress in her voice, "you must have known a young lady who lived with her. Her name was Meta."

"Yes, we knew her," he answered quietly. "Are you a relation of hers?"

"No." Elsie turned to him with a sudden lighting-up of her face. "But she is a great deal to me! And you really knew her?"

"We knew her," he repeated, "while she lived. Her story was a sad one. I thought you were related to her because you are like her."

"Like her?" Elsie echoed. "I must have grown like her through thinking about her so much! But I never saw her in my life."

The man still looked at her, with a glance kind as well as penetrating. "I daresay my mother will be ready to have a chat with you," he said, after a moment's pause. "Excuse me; I will go and speak to her again."

She waited, looking out through the doorway, and feeling that she was nearer the goal than she had ever been before. A strange joy and excitement thrilled her as she heard the shopkeeper returning.

"My mother will be glad to see you, madam," he said.

As he spoke she caught the gleam of firelight in a room at the back of the shop. It was a neat little parlour in which the old lady sat, and she rose to receive her visitor with quiet courtesy. Elsie sat down in an arm-chair, close to the window overlooking a little back-yard, and Mrs. Beaton attentively studied her face as she spoke.

"My son tells me that you want to ask some questions about Mrs. Penn and Miss Neale."

Elsie started slightly.

"Miss Neale?" she repeated. "Ah, that must be Meta."

"Did you not know her as Miss Neale?" the old lady asked.

"I only knew her as Meta. I found a manuscript of hers in the drawer of an old table in my lodgings, and I have been seeking her ever since. That search has brought me to you."

"A manuscript? Did it tell you her story fully? Was it long or short? She had not time to write much, I think, in her last days."

"It was not long; only the outlines of her story were told. The manuscript began with the words, 'If I only knew that some one would be kind to Jamie,' and ever since I read them I have been longing to find Jamie and be kind to him."

Mrs. Beaton had put on her spectacles, and was regarding the speaker with an intent gaze.

"Do you know," she said, after a pause, "that you don't seem a stranger to me? You are like Miss Neale—so much like her that you might pass for her sister. Many a time she has sat where you are sitting now."

"It is as I thought," Elsie murmured. "I have been guided by a vanished hand."

The old lady smiled.

"We are all guided," she said; "but sometimes the guidance is more plainly manifested than usual, or it may be that our perceptions are quickened. You will be disappointed when I tell you that I don't know where Jamie is now. However, you must keep up your heart, and not be discouraged."

"I will not be discouraged," Elsie answered resolutely. "Did Mrs. Penn take the boy away with her?"

"She did. She went away more than a year ago, and she has not fulfilled her promise of writing to me. If I had not been old and rheumatic I would have kept the little fellow myself."

"I wish you had kept him," Elsie said earnestly. "But until he is safe in my own keeping I shall not rest."

"That was spoken like Miss Neale," the old lady remarked. "You are prettier than she was; I am an old woman, and you won't mind my plain speaking. She was not as tall as you are, and her eyes were grey instead of brown, as yours are; but she had your black lashes and eyebrows. She always wore a very peaceful look, a look that comes to some people after great suffering. Your face is more eager than hers."

"Mrs. Beaton," said Elsie, bending forward entreatingly, "I want to hear Meta's story from one who knew her. She has said very little about herself in her manuscript. Won't you begin at once, and tell me all that you know?"

"Yes, my dear, I will tell you," Mrs. Beaton replied. "I have missed her very much. She used to come and talk to me when she had a little time to spare. Hers was a busy life, and it was a life lived for others. She was always going about among the burden-bearers, and trying to lighten the burdens. That was how it was that she met Mr. Waring."

CHAPTER VI

HAROLD AND META

> "The dear Lord's best interpreters
> Are humble human souls;
> The gospel of a life like hers
> Is more than books or scrolls.
> From scheme and creed the light goes out,
> The saintly fact survives;
> The blessed Master none can doubt
> Revealed in holy lives."
>
> —Whitier.

The two women, sitting together in the little parlour behind the shop, seemed to have been drawn to each other by some subtle influence which neither could explain. When Mrs. Beaton proposed that Elsie should take off her cloak and stay long enough to drink a cup of tea, the invitation was accepted at once. And then Elsie told her name, and a little bit of her own history, before she began to listen to the story of Meta.

"There is a resemblance between your life and hers," Mrs. Beaton said thoughtfully. "I remember she once told me that she was alone in the world; parents, brothers, and sisters had all passed away, and the few relations who remained cared nothing about her. Some artist friend, who had helped her to get on, recommended Mrs. Penn as a safe woman to live with. Then, too, that top room was a suitable place to work in; there was plenty of light and air. One day Mrs. Penn brought her here, and asked my son to show her some of our art treasures, and that is how we were acquainted with her first."

"Was she very clever?" Elsie asked.

"I don't know enough of art to answer you; but my son says that she was. Andrew is a judge in such matters, and I have often heard him say that Miss Neale had the true gift. But, although she had been well trained, she lacked a good many of those advantages which help to make artists successful. She could not afford to travel, and she was so poor that she was forced to work below her powers. Still, she was rising steadily in her calling, and increasing her earnings, when she first met Mr. Waring."

"Mr. Waring? Ah, that was Harold," said Elsie.

"Yes, that was Harold. He was the junior curate at St. Lucy's Church in a street close by. In that street there was a young girl dying of consumption who was very lonely, and wanted a good deal of cheering and visiting. I used to see her as often as I could; but when my rheumatism cripples me I am helpless. I soon found out that Miss Neale knew how to comfort the sick, and I asked her to go to the poor girl. She went, and did more good than I had ever done. And it was in that sick-room that Mr. Waring first spoke to her."

Elsie recalled the words in the manuscript, "What a new life came to me all at once when I met Harold for the first time!"

"There are many kinds of love," continued the old woman in her quiet voice, "and it was given to those two to know the best kind of all. They gained strength from each other; they worked as one. In these crowded streets they have left traces of their simple, earnest lives—lives of self-sacrifice and devotion to humanity. They made no noise in the world. Harold Waring was not eloquent; he was not a profound scholar; he said very little about creeds. And yet all sorts of believers and unbelievers trusted this man, and looked up to him, because he was simply an interpreter of Divine love. Harold and Meta lived long enough to reveal their Master's sweetness to the people. And the sweetness lingers with us still."

Mrs. Beaton took off her spectacles and wiped her eyes. Then she looked up at Elsie with a smile, and shook her head over her own weakness. "My tears are for myself—not for them," she said. "I still miss them, and I am too old to go amongst those who miss them even more than I do. I shall never forget Mr. Waring's face when he came to tell me about the legacy. He was tall and fair, with clear eyes that had the blue of heaven in them."

"And Jamie's eyes are like his," interrupted Elsie.

"Yes; that's true. The boy was more like his uncle than his father. I only saw Mr. James Waring once or twice, and I always distrusted him. Well, as I was saying, Harold Waring's face was beautiful with hope and happiness. 'We shall have a home, Mrs. Beaton,' he said; 'we shall have a home!'"

"That hope was never realised!" sighed Elsie.

Mrs. Beaton's look was very bright.

"Don't you think that it is realised now?" she asked. "I have often fancied that it is the want unanswered here which is most fully satisfied hereafter. It makes the new life all the fresher and sweeter, you see. They wanted a home; but home is not a place, it is a state. There can be no home at all if there is not that mystical house, 'not made with hands,' where spirits blend and dwell together for ever."

Just then the parlour-door opened quietly, and Andrew Beaton came into the room. "Mother is giving you some of her notions," he said. "She says that all the joys of heaven must first have had their beginnings in our souls on earth."

"'To him that hath, shall be given,'" the old lady quoted. "Miss Kilner, I'm afraid you find me very wearisome, my dear. You wanted to hear about Meta Neale's life in this world, and I am trying to talk about her life in the next. Forgive a foolish old woman, who sits and dreams over her fire."

It was pleasant to see the look in Andrew's eyes when his mother called herself a foolish old woman. His glance had flatly contradicted her statement before Elsie spoke.

"Mrs. Beaton," she said earnestly, "I like to hear your notions. You have done me good. I have been thinking a great deal too much lately about the things that are temporal. There were no spiritual influences in my Sussex home," she added, with a sigh.

"One ought to look up sometimes," said Andrew; "but one mustn't forget the story of that great artist who was painting the ceiling of a chapel for two years. He got into such a confirmed habit of looking up that it cost him a mighty effort to look down at the common ground he had to walk on."

Mrs. Beaton poured out tea for her son, and smiled at Elsie across the table. It was a humble home at the back of a London shop, but Elsie found here the thought and refinement which she had so often missed in other houses. She remembered the prattle which usually accompanied the clatter of afternoon teacups, and the bits of scandal handed round with the cake.

"I don't think we will dwell too long on the end of Meta's earthly love-story," said Mrs. Beaton, after a pause; "she has told you enough in her manuscript. For nearly a year after Harold Waring died she was living and working among us, and taking care of Jamie. It was in December—just before Christmas—that Mrs. Penn found her by the child's side in her last sleep."

There was another pause. Elsie felt that tears were gathering in her eyes and could not speak. It was well that Andrew broke the silence.

"It is just a year and six months since Mrs. Penn and Jamie went away," he said. "She had grown tired of her house, I think, and the death of Miss Neale preyed upon her mind. Some one came and took house and furniture off her hands. My mother and I have been expecting a letter, but no letter has come."

"I think we ought to bestir ourselves," the old lady remarked. "Mrs. Penn was not quite the right person to have the care of a boy. If I hadn't believed that we should be informed of her movements, I would not have let Jamie go so easily. But the child clung to her very much after Miss Neale's death; no one else could comfort him."

"Have you ever heard of Arnold Wayne?" Elsie suddenly asked.

"Never," replied both the Beatons at once. "Who was he? Had he anything to do with Miss Neale?"

"I don't think she ever saw him," Elsie replied. "Her manuscript merely says that he was Harold's college friend, and she must search Harold's papers to find his address. It was evident that she felt her own end approaching, and thought that Mr. Wayne might do something for Jamie."

Andrew Beaton caught at the idea at once. "We'll find him out!" he cried. "Mr. Waring was a King's College man. It will be easy enough to learn something about Arnold Wayne there. But we must find Jamie first of all."

"Don't you know where Mrs. Penn went when she left Soho Square?" inquired Elsie.

"Not exactly," Andrew admitted. "Mother, how could we have been so neglectful? We ought to have insisted on having her address!"

"But she had no address to give us," Mrs. Beaton answered, with a troubled look on her kind face. "She said she would go to stay with some friends at Brighton for a month; the sea-air would be good for the boy and herself. They had both fretted themselves quite ill. After leaving Brighton she was thinking of settling at Lee, in Kent. Naturally, I approved of the Brighton plan, as I knew that Jamie needed a change."

Elsie was thoughtful for a moment; then she looked up, with a sudden hope shining in her eyes. "Perhaps we are worrying ourselves without a cause," she said. "It may be that they have not left Brighton, and the child is well and happy there."

"Who can tell?" The words came from Andrew as he rose from his chair and went to a side-table. "I am going to write to Mrs. Penn

through the papers." His mother and Elsie watched him as he opened a blotting-book and set about his task at once. There was something firm and business-like in his way of doing things. In a few minutes the notice was written, and he read it aloud to them: —
"Mrs. Penn, formerly of — Soho Square, is requested to communicate at once with Andrew Beaton, — Wardour Street, W."

"That will do," said Mrs. Beaton approvingly.

Elsie, too, rose from her seat. The afternoon was wearing away, and Miss Saxon would be getting uneasy at her absence.

"You will come again, my dear?" said the old lady, holding her hand in a lingering clasp.

"I shall be very glad to come," Elsie answered. "It is so long since I have talked with any one so motherly as you are." As she spoke her lips quivered. They both knew that the loss of a mother leaves a void which can only be filled up in heaven, and perhaps the first treasure restored to us there will be the unspeakable gift of a mother's love.

"I have never had a daughter," said Mrs. Beaton, with a slight trembling in her voice. "When Meta Neale came I sometimes caught a glimpse of what a daughter might be."

The room was growing darker, but Elsie felt rather than saw the swift look of pain which swept across Andrew's face. She felt in her mind, magnetically, the feeling that was in his. It came to her all at once — that sudden, strange intuition which reveals to us the deep places in other people's lives.

He, too, had caught a glimpse of what a daughter might have been to his mother. He had seen how lovely his life might have grown if he could have won Meta. But that vision had been sternly put away from him; neither in this life nor the next would she belong to him.

It was worse than a loss, Elsie thought. It was "the devotion to something afar" from his own sphere — a longing for the light of a star that had never shone into his world at all. He was not grieving for a gift given and taken away, but for a treasure which had never for an instant come within his reach. She went away in the gathering dusk with a heart full of sympathy. Had the "vanished hand" guided her into the path of his solitary life that she might shed a ray of brightness there?

Miss Saxon was waiting for her with an anxious face. Some people had called and left cards—friends who had lived once near her old neighbourhood. Elsie felt very little interest in them now; her mind was full of new feelings; she did not care to talk over bygone days. "I don't want to begin visiting," she said. "I am so busy, Miss Saxon! In this life of mine there is so much to do—is there not?"

CHAPTER VII

MRS. PENN

> "I have a boy of five years old,
> His face is fair and fresh to see,
> His limbs are cast in beauty's mould,
> And dearly he loves me."
>
> —Wordsworth.

Three days went by, and then Elsie bent her steps to Wardour Street again. Andrew Beaton was in his old place behind the counter, but his face did not look any brighter than usual.

"No answer yet, Miss Kilner," he said. "My mother is worried about the matter. She thinks that we have neglected a duty. I am glad you have come. She is too much alone."

Elsie found the old lady sitting dejectedly in her little parlour, but she brightened at the sight of her visitor.

"We have heard nothing," she began. "And yet the notice has been in all the papers. Mrs. Penn was always a newspaper reader; nothing escaped her eyes. I am beginning to fear that she is dead."

"We mustn't imagine evils," Elsie replied.

"But if she is dead, one doesn't know what may have happened to the boy! Mrs. Penn had friends and relatives, but would they be likely to look after him? That's what I have said to Andrew a dozen times at least."

She took off her spectacles with fingers that trembled a little, and put her work into an old-fashioned basket with a crimson lining. Elsie had gentle ways with old people, knowing instinctively how to soothe them with touch and voice. She poured out tea, and hovered round Mrs. Beaton with little attentions which were like caresses.

Andrew, coming in with his quiet step, gave Miss Kilner a look and a word of gratitude.

If you set out to do a good deed, you may do a hundred small kindnesses on the way. Elsie's quest seemed very likely to prove fruitless, but in the seeking she was scattering flowers as she went along. Andrew, who sometimes found his life sadly commonplace, picked up a blossom or two, and wore them thankfully. The street, the shop, and the parlour were all touched and beautified by these little graces which a woman like Elsie bestows spontaneously.

It was a pleasant tea-drinking in the London parlour, although the sun could send in only a slanting beam or two.

They had, all three, talked themselves into a hopeful mood. In their brightened fancy Jamie was already found, and they were beginning to arrange his future destiny. Elsie proceeded to state her views on the education of boys; but, as she had never had any boys to educate, those views were rather vague. Mrs. Beaton expressed a wish that he could be turned into a blue-coat boy; his curly golden head was so pretty that it was almost a sin to cover it with a cap, and he would soon grow used to being without one. Andrew hoped that he wouldn't be spoiled, and made into a milksop, and suggested that he ought to be taught a useful trade as soon as possible.

Elsie had other ideas; she wanted him to be sent to college.

Mrs. Beaton said it would be a shame to set him to work too early; he was only a little more than five years old. Both women thought that Andrew was too severe in his notions about boys.

Andrew thought that many a good lad was spoilt because he had lacked a man's control.

Elsie thought that many a dear little fellow was half-brutalised because he had lacked a woman's influence.

Mrs. Beaton then felt that it was her turn to make a remark, but no one ever heard the words of wisdom which were about to issue from her lips. Quite suddenly, with unusual noise, the parlour door was flung open, and a woman rushed into the room.

Andrew started to his feet. Elsie, who had just taken up the tea-pot, set it down again upon the table. Mrs. Beaton pushed back her cap-ribbons with both hands, and uttered a little shriek.

"It's Mrs. Penn!" she cried. "Oh, Mrs. Penn, it is you, isn't it? And you're gone clean out of your mind, aren't you? Oh, dear! oh, dear!"

"Yes," answered the intruder distractedly, "it is me. And I'm gone clean out of my mind."

"We don't want you without your mind," said Andrew, grown suddenly discourteous. "If you are mad you ought not to have come. Don't you see that you have given my mother a terrible shock?"

"Don't be unkind, Mr. Beaton!" exclaimed Elsie, in a tone of re-proof. "Of course Mrs. Penn has come to bring us some news. Oh, Mrs. Penn," she added, losing dignity and self-control all at once, "do speak one word and tell us what has become of Jamie!"

For a moment it seemed as if Mrs. Penn had no power to comply with this simple request. She stood gaping at them all; then, sud-denly flinging up her hands with a despairing gesture, she panted out, "Lost!"

Mrs. Beaton sank back in her chair with eyes closed. Andrew bent over his mother, holding a smelling-bottle to her nostrils, and mur-muring reassuring words. Elsie was very pale.

The old lady recovered herself, sat up, and said, rather feebly, that there was nothing the matter. Andrew, somewhat relieved, darted an angry glance at Mrs. Penn.

"Pray sit down, Mrs. Penn," he said, "and let me beg you to be composed. Perhaps a cup of tea may steady your nerves."

Elsie poured out the tea at once, and handed it kindly to the poor shaken woman, whose distress was very genuine.

"The *Daily Telegraph* told me to come here. That's why I came," she whimpered at last. "But no one seems glad to see me," she added tearfully.

Andrew felt a pang of self-reproach.

"We are very glad," he said promptly. "If I was rude I hope you will pardon me. But mother can't stand a shock, and you came upon us rather suddenly, you see."

"I'm so unhappy," poor Mrs. Penn replied. "I daresay I don't seem a bit like myself. I lost him nine weeks ago."

Elsie gave a little exclamation of dismay. Had the guidance of the vanished hand led only to a disappointment like this?

"I wish you had told us sooner," said Andrew, trying to suppress his indignation.

"The weeks have gone by like a whirlwind, and my head's been in a mist ever since I lost him," Mrs. Penn declared, wiping her eyes.

"Are you sure that your head wasn't in a mist before you lost him?" asked Mrs. Beaton, with unwonted sternness.

Something in the tone of the questioner led Elsie to examine Mrs. Penn with closer attention. She was a woman of sixty, who had evidently been healthy and active in her earlier days, and ought to have been strong and capable still. But there was a redness of the eyes, and a certain pink puffiness of the whole countenance which had a suspicious look.

"My health hasn't been good lately," she said, in her whimpering voice. "No one knows the burden that the boy has been to me, but I couldn't find it in my heart to part with him."

"If you had written to us, as you promised to do, we would have relieved you of the burden," Mrs. Beaton replied.

"I've been going to write hundreds of times, only I'm such a bad letter-writer. And then I've intended to come and see you, but I've put off coming because things always seemed to prevent me. We stayed at Brighton three months; I don't like Brighton. I was glad to get nearer to London."

"Where did you go when you left Brighton?" Andrew inquired.

"We came up to Lee. My niece Maria is married to a market-gardener there, a Mr. Dennett; he's a most respectable man, and he took quite a fancy to Jamie. But Maria has no children, and she doesn't care for boys; they seem to worry her."

"And between you and Maria the poor little fellow was neglected," cried Mrs. Beaton, in a tremor of anger.

"Don't say so; pray, don't say so; it hurts my feelings dreadfully," wailed Mrs. Penn. "I'm sure I paid regularly for him and myself, and he always had enough to eat. But, as Maria has often said, it's a troublesome thing to have a child on your hands."

"How did you lose him?" Mrs. Beaton asked. She steadied her voice as well as she could, but there was an angry light in her kind old eyes.

"I didn't lose him. He lost himself. He must have wandered away somewhere," said this exasperating woman, beginning to cry again. "We went to the police, and did all we could to find him, but we never caught a glimpse of him any more. After wearing myself out for nine weeks, I saw your notice in the *Daily Telegraph*, and then I thought you must have found him. I came here all in a hurry, with my heart full of hope."

There was nothing more to be extracted from her. It was clear that she had told all she could tell.

Elsie turned to Andrew with a look of distress more eloquent than words. As he met the sorrowful gaze of her beautiful dark eyes, a light seemed suddenly to flash from his, and he spoke out in a resolute tone.

"Don't be afraid that I shall let the grass grow under my feet, Miss Kilner. I shall go to Scotland Yard at once," he said, rising and buttoning his coat.

He merely lingered to ask Mrs. Penn a few rapid questions about the boy's dress and general appearance, and then the door closed behind him, and he was gone.

There was a moment of silence; then Elsie, rising from her chair, went over to Mrs. Beaton and kissed her.

"I am going home now," she whispered. "We won't despair yet. I shall try to be hopeful."

But her attempts at hopefulness were of little avail, and she hurried out of Wardour Street, holding her head down, crying as she went. She walked swiftly, never once slackening her speed till she had gained her own door. And inside the house she seemed to lose all courage and strength and faith, and fell sobbing into Miss Saxon's arms.

"Oh," she said, "it is all in vain! Jamie is lost, utterly lost, and only his angel knows where to find him!"

CHAPTER VIII

LOOKING AT PICTURES

"A quiet and weary woman,
With all her illusions flown."

—A. A. Proctor.

About this time, when there was nothing to do but to stand and wait, Elsie occupied herself chiefly with books.

One little bit of literary work (which will live, I suppose, as long as literature endures) particularly engaged her attention in these days. It was "Dream-Children" in the "Essays of Elia."

She had so accustomed herself to the imaginary companionship of Jamie that she found it almost impossible to live without him. At nights she had fallen into a habit of glancing towards that corner of her large bedroom in which his little bed was to stand. There was the golden head burying its fluffy curls in the pillow; there was the dimpled hand lying outside the quilt.

And now the dream was fast fading away into a still fainter dream. Jamie had vanished; it was most likely, she thought, that he was dead; anyhow, it was only a miracle which could ever restore him to those who mourned for him. He had joined that troop of phantom children who come to us in our lonely hours, saying, "We are nothing, less than nothing, and dreams. We are only what might have been, and must wait upon the tedious shores of Lethe millions of ages before we have existence and a name."

Meanwhile she lived very much as other people live, and grew prettier every day, gaining beauty in the sad and dreamy peace of her daily life. Calm will work wonders for a woman who has been fretted and worried for years, and this is the reason why some are far more beautiful in their autumn than in their summer or their spring.

The shade of melancholy, which always hung over Elsie now, added a new charm to her face. In her girlhood she had been too eager, too vivid; she had lacked the subtle sweetness of repose. People who met her nowadays invariably noticed her tranquillity: some envied, and all admired it.

She made acquaintances, and went out sometimes, and wherever she went she left an impression. If she was a trifle too indifferent to please everybody, she seldom made an enemy. Women instinctively understood that she did not want to be their rival. Men felt that the gentle unconsciousness, which nullified their pretty speeches, was really the result of preoccupation. She was always gracious, always kind; but no one could ever get very near to her heart.

She went often to sit with Mrs. Beaton in the little parlour behind the shop. Here there was real work to be done—the quiet work of cheering an old woman who had never known a daughter's love. Sometimes the blessing withheld in youth is granted in old age. Mrs. Beaton had received much from Meta, but Meta had been worn with the warfare of a hard life. Elsie had more leisure to give her a daughter's tenderness.

Andrew Beaton had strained every nerve, but had found no trace of the missing boy. He had been to Lee, and had seen Dennett, the green-grocer, and his wife, and had satisfied himself that they were seldom sober enough to attend to anything. Poor Mrs. Penn's habit of intemperance had been strengthened by her connection with these people. Andrew gave up the Dennetts and Mrs. Penn as a hopeless set.

Spring days grew warmer and brighter; shop-windows were gay with all the colours of the rainbow; women moved about in pretty, delicate dresses, looking like animated flowers.

Miss Saxon reminded Elsie that young women ought not to go out habited in black gowns when the white and purple clover blossoms stood thick in the meadows, and the hawthorn shook its fragrant snows over the hedges. So Elsie dressed herself in violet and lilac, and Miss Saxon secretly exulted in seeing the admiring glances which were cast upon her when she went out into the sunshine.

One day Miss Kilner went to the Royal Academy Exhibition with a very old friend.

This old friend was Mr. Lennard, rector of the Sussex village where she was born. He was seventy years of age—hale, rosy, and strong; a suitable escort for the beautiful young woman who wore a bonnet made of heliotrope, and had dark-brown eyes that shone like stars.

She enjoyed the pictures with all her heart, especially those views of cornfields steeped in yellow sunlight, and glimpses of shady woodland which reminded her of her early home. Mr. Lennard, too, enjoyed the pictures, but they did not absorb his whole attention. Now and then he caught sight of familiar faces in the crowd, and then there were hearty greetings and rapid questions and answers.

Sometimes it was the face of an old college friend which caught his eye, and he would almost shout for joy to see it smiling and alive, when he had thought it hidden under the daisies. Sometimes it was a rosy matron whom he had last seen as a bashful bride. And these meetings were so frequent that Elsie had got quite used to his starts and exclamations before they had gone half through the rooms.

When he said, "Bless me, it's—no, it isn't—yes, it is—of course it is!" she was gazing intently at one of those pictures which will always have an attraction for women of her temperament. Long afterwards she could have described the painting accurately, and would never forget it as long as she lived.

Two nuns, one old and the other young, were waiting for admittance outside the door of a convent. They had been out into the world to nurse the sick, and had returned (each laden with her basket) in the glory of a summer morning. The elder woman, weary with her labours, waited with half-closed eyes for the door to open. The younger, pale, but full of irrepressible vitality, stood looking at the rich, warm human life which she had renounced for ever. A young wife, with an infant on her arm, had brought her husband his midday meal, and he had flung down his scythe to kiss her under the trees. Those two faces, browned with the sun, flushed with the bloom of the flower, seemed the natural product of the beautiful earth. You could almost hear the myriad sounds of summer; waters trickling through the moss and roots of the wood, the hum of bees, the birds' joyous songs. The very sunlight seemed to dance for gladness among the leaf-shadows as it played over the grey garb of the Sisters. But you knew that in another moment the door would open and close again, shutting out all these common human joys — kisses and smiles and signs of that everyday bliss which makes a paradise of simple lives.

Now Elsie, in her loneliness, had had her dreams of the convent. But a picture of this kind was a better warning than any sermon which a hot-headed Protestant ever preached. There are natures which can put forth blossoms, pale and sweet, in the air of the cloister, and there are others which can flower only in the atmosphere of the world.

The pity is that the women meant for the world too often fly to the cloister, and the women who would have made admirable nuns —

> "Devout and pure,
> Sober, steadfast, and demure,"

persist in taking upon themselves those duties of wifehood and maternity for which they were never fitted at all.

Elsie had a rich heart, but its outpourings seemed to be thrown back upon herself, and she had sometimes longed to hide her disappointment in seclusion. But the picture spoke to her, as pictures can do. True art can often succeed where divinity fails; the painter preaches more effectually than the parson.

She gazed at the nuns, quite unconscious that she herself made a picture, and that some one was gazing intently at her. Then, slowly realising that Mr. Lennard had found another acquaintance, she turned, and met the earnest look of a pair of deep-blue eyes.

They were uncommon eyes, singularly blue, singularly true. Their owner was a tall man, much bronzed, and not regularly handsome; but he had that knightliness of look and bearing which always wins notice and attracts liking. Although he wore the prosaic garb of the period, there was something about him that suggested Camelot, and Arthur's court; something that recalled Lancelot, and Galahad, and Percivale; something, in short, which appealed to the romantic side of Elsie's nature. So these two young persons looked at each other, but it did not occur to Mr. Lennard that they might possibly like to get acquainted.

Moreover, it was near the luncheon hour, and the rector had promised to take Elsie to a house in Park Lane. He shook hands heartily with the knightly stranger, reminded Elsie of their engagement, and began to make his way through the crowd to the door.

In the whirl and roar of Piccadilly he tried to say something about that unexpected meeting, but part of his sentence was lost.

"— —since he was a lad. Even now I can scarcely recall his name. My memory begins to play strange tricks. Donald—no—Ronald. Ronald—what? I can't get further than Ronald; my head is a trifle confused to-day. Coming up from the country, you know. That's our 'bus, isn't it? All right."

They went to Park Lane, but not another word was said about Ronald, and on the following day Mr. Lennard returned to Sussex.

The summer advanced; Elsie accepted invitations now and then; but it soon became evident to Miss Saxon that she did not care very much for society.

She took a deep interest in all that concerned the welfare of children. She went to public meetings and heard grand things spoken

on their behalf; she learnt what true, large-hearted men, with power, and education, and opportunity, were doing for little ones in the
world, and all the while the thought of Jamie lay deep down in her
heart. He was never forgotten.

Nor did the Beatons forget him, but every effort to trace him had
failed.

They often talked of him with Elsie as they sat, all three, in the little room behind the shop. Some subtle influence always seemed to
draw Miss Kilner's steps to Wardour Street, and her presence was
welcome there.

CHAPTER IX

MEETINGS

"Such a deal of wonder is broken out within this hour that ballad-
makers cannot be able to express it."
—*A Winter's Tale.*

Poor Mrs. Penn had a conscience. It had been lulled to sleep while
she lived an unwholesome life with Maria and her husband, and
allowed herself to be dominated by them. But the loss of Jamie and
the visit to Wardour Street had awakened her better nature and the
feelings of a happier time. She recalled Harold Waring's faithful
words and Meta Neale's gentle counsels, and remembered all the
comfort and help which she had found in Mrs. Beaton's friendship.

So powerfully did good emotions work within her that she suddenly resolved to fly from Maria's companionship. The Dennetts
were mortally offended, but what did that matter? She wanted to go
back to her old haunts and be helped by the presence of those who
could lift her out of miry ways; and Mrs. Beaton and her son took
compassion upon the repentant woman, and let her come to live
with them. Sometimes they made little excursions into the suburbs,
which did them all good. Mrs. Penn became a really useful member
of the household, and waited on Mrs. Beaton with careful attention.
Andrew, who had been troubled about his mother's increasing fee-
bleness, was no longer afraid to see her go out of doors. Mrs. Penn
was by her side, a trustworthy companion nowadays, with a stout
arm which could be safely leant upon.

July was gloriously bright, and one day the two women—Mrs. Beaton and Mrs. Penn—had prepared themselves for a trip to Richmond, when Miss Kilner suddenly presented herself.

"One longs to escape from London to-day," she said. "So you are going to Richmond? I have a school-friend who lives down by the river, and I told Miss Saxon that I should go to see her."

"Will you come with us?" Mrs. Beaton asked, brightening.

"Yes," Elsie answered; and the three went off together.

Down by the river there are old houses set deep in leafy gardens; creepers hang drowsily in the delicious air; long aisles open upon terraces bright with flowers. It was in an earthly paradise of this kind that Elsie loitered away a golden afternoon; and then, when the clocks were striking six, she went off to rejoin her companions.

She found them at the appointed meeting-place, and they all walked up from the river-side through a lane opening into the highway of the town. Mrs. Beaton, a little weary, moved slowly, leaning on Mrs. Penn. Elsie, a few steps in the rear, gave herself up to one of those reveries which so often come to us at the close of a summer day. The lights were golden on the river. Some people were singing in a boat, and the voices floated sweetly over the water; it was pleasant melody, but there was a faint tone of sadness in the strain.

An open carriage and pair waited under the overhanging trees in the lane. Leaning back lazily on the cushions was a lady, fair and still young, with a beautiful boy by her side. The child was in high spirits; his laugh rang out clear and fresh as Elsie drew near. He stood up in the carriage in his pretty sailor's suit, and the low sunlight shone into his blooming face and blue eyes. At the sight of him Mrs. Penn stopped short and uttered a little cry.

"It's Jamie!" she exclaimed. "It's really Jamie!"

The boy knew her voice; the laugh died out on his lips in an instant; he looked at her with a gaze half-frightened, half-defiant, and drew closer to the lady's side.

"What is the matter, dear?" they heard her ask.

Before he could reply, before any one could speak again, a terrible thing happened. The horses began to plunge violently, and then, as the drowsy coachman woke with a start, they set off at a mad pace in spite of all his efforts to control them. Down the lane they went at a wild gallop, their thundering hoofs raising a cloud of dust, and the three horror-stricken women caught a swift glimpse of the lady and the child clinging to each other in a despairing embrace.

Scarcely knowing what she was doing, Elsie began to run after the flying carriage at the top of her speed; Mrs. Penn followed her at a slower pace, and poor Mrs. Beaton came panting behind.

Miss Kilner was slight of figure and light of foot, and eagerness seemed to lend her wings. She was still getting over the ground at a rapid rate, when she saw the dust-cloud vanish, and perceived that the carriage had come to a stand-still. Was the danger, then, over? Her heart gave a throb of passionate thankfulness as she pressed on, longing to assure herself that Jamie was safe, and to hold him, for one brief moment even, in her arms.

One or two watermen had come up and gathered round the panting horses. The coachman, white and shaky, was talking and gesticulating; his mistress, looking very fair in her faintness, had been helped out of the carriage by a tall man with a brown face.

Elsie, as she came up breathless to this group, took in two facts at once. Jamie was safe and unhurt, and the brown-faced man was Mr. Lennard's friend Ronald. He looked every inch a knight, as he stood there in his suit of fresh, white flannels, his bronzed face with a summer glow in it, and the dark hair cropped close to his head. The lady, in a silvery voice that faltered once or twice, was pouring out her thanks. Elsie comprehended it all in a moment; it was Ronald who had stopped the horses, and saved, perhaps, two lives.

"I cannot trust them again," the lady said, glancing at the handsome chestnuts with a shudder. "We had better go home in the train."

The boy was holding her hand, and pressing close to the folds of her dainty gown. Elsie came up to them, very pale, with a light in her eyes. Her glance rested on the little lad, and she stretched out her hand to him with an impulsive gesture. "Oh," she said, "it is

Jamie Waring, and I have been trying to find him for weeks and weeks! I have no right to claim him, I know; but I have wanted him for such a long, long time. To see him safe and well, after such a weary search— —"

She broke off abruptly. The brown man was standing in front of her with his eyes fixed on her face; he was gazing at her so earnestly, sincerely, and wistfully that for an instant she almost lost herself. Jamie's gaze was less sympathetic; he looked puzzled, and kept very close to his protectress.

"I found Jamie with some organ-grinders," said the lady, recovering her composure, and speaking in rather a cold voice. "The organ-woman was beating him, and I stopped my carriage to interfere. They were in a quiet road near Lee, and of course there was no policeman to be seen. I asked the child if he belonged to these people, and he cried, 'No, no!' and clung to me. I saw that he was not dirty and neglected; his clothes were rather poor, but there was nothing of the tramp about him. To make a long story short, I fell in love with you—didn't I, Jamie?—and so I took you home with me and waited for you to be claimed, but no one ever claimed you."

Her fair face softened as she looked down at the child, and her voice grew tender when she spoke to him. He still stood clasping her hand and resting his head against her dress.

"He has no relations," Elsie said. "No one has any right to take him from you."

Mrs. Penn, flushed and half-sobbing, came up at this moment, and she, too, extended her arms to the boy. But at the sight of her he drew himself up to his full height and waved his hand with the majesty of a little king. "Go away!" he said. "Go away home!"

"Oh, Jamie!" she cried; "aren't you glad to see me again?"

"No!" he answered, with another wave of the dimpled hand. "I don't love you a bit! You let Maria beat me. I hate Maria. I won't come with you!"

For a moment no one spoke. The brown man was evidently much amused by the little scene, and looked at the boy with undisguised approval.

"Was this child left in your charge?" the lady asked, addressing Mrs. Penn with cold severity.

"There was no one to take him, madam," the crestfallen woman replied. "He was living with Miss Neale, who was a lodger of mine, and she died, quite suddenly, in my house. His father— —"

"His father had deserted him." It was Mrs. Beaton who spoke. She had reached the little group, and having but a poor opinion of her friend's eloquence, she took up the tale herself. "But Jamie Waring is well connected, madam; his uncle was our clergyman, the Reverend Harold Waring, curate of St. Lucy's, in Berwick Street, and— —"

"Harold Waring! Why, he was a dear old friend of mine!" Mrs. Beaton was interrupted in her turn, and it was the man in flannels who cut her story short. "If I had only known that Waring had left a nephew alone in the world I should have claimed him," he went on, with a ring of determination in his voice. "My name is Wayne— Arnold Wayne—you may have heard Mr. Waring speak of me?"

"Yes, sir, we have," Mrs. Beaton replied. "Here is Miss Kilner, who found your name in poor Miss Neale's manuscript. Miss Neale, sir, was engaged to be married to Mr. Waring."

"He wrote to tell me of his engagement," said Arnold Wayne, looking at Elsie. "What a complicated business this is! It seems that we each have an interest in this young gentleman," he added, with a smile at the fair lady.

"Mr. Wayne!" exclaimed Jamie's protectress, in her silvery voice. "We were to have met at Rushbrook last October, and you didn't come. I was staying with your cousins the Danforths. I am Mrs. Verdon."

"I'm delighted to meet you at last," he said cordially. "Mary and Lily were always talking about you. Isn't all this extraordinary? There never was anything like it in a three-volume novel!"

Then they both laughed with a comfortable air of old acquaint-anceship, and Elsie suddenly had a sense of being left out in the cold.

CHAPTER X

LONELINESS

> "While I! I sat alone and watched;
> My lot in life, to live alone,
> In mine own world of interests,
> Much felt, but little shown."

> —Christina Rossetti.

Yes; Elsie felt as if she were left out in the cold, and she looked as if she felt it.

There are women to whom nature has granted the gift of silent emotion. They have mobile faces, changeful eyes, soft lips, which express joy or desolation naturally, and with the charm of perfect simplicity and truth. These women keep their youth a long time; every experience of life comes to them with the freshness of a first feeling; they retain the capacity to rejoice and suffer to the very end of their days. Men like them, because they find them real, and because these impressionable characters have the attraction of varying often. Anything is more tolerable than monotony.

Arnold Wayne looked from Mrs. Verdon to Elsie, and read a pathetic story in her brown eyes.

"May I introduce myself, Miss Kilner?" he said. "I have heard of you so often from Mr. Lennard."

This was a fib. For years he had not seen or heard anything of the rector; but it was a fib which slipped from him unawares. He had wished for an introduction to Elsie when he had seen her at the picture gallery with the old clergyman, and he had secretly anathematised Mr. Lennard's obtuseness. He was not going to lose a second chance, he said to himself.

"I have known the Lennards all my life," Elsie answered. "They belong to my old home. It is a great pleasure to see thc rector when he comes to town."

Mrs. Verdon regarded the speaker quietly, with the practised glance of a woman of the world; and she listened to the refined voice and accent with critical ears. It would be safe, she decided, to notice this stranger.

"Will you come and see Jamie some day?" she said, addressing Elsie in her silvery voice, which could be very sweet when she wished to please. "I am a widow without children, myself, and I want to know how you came to take such an interest in him. Go and kiss that lady, Jamie; you must learn to know her quite well."

The boy obeyed without reluctance. He had listened attentively to all that had been said, and, being an intelligent child, had come to the conclusion that no one wanted to take him away from Mrs. Verdon.

Elsie kissed the blooming face uplifted to hers, and pressed him in her arms for a moment. He was the child of her dreams, presented to her now in substantial form; but he was not meant for her. She could never have him for her own.

But it was the little lad's good, and not her own pleasure, which she had been seeking. Meta's prayers were answered; somebody was kind to Jamie.

Only, why had the vanished hand pointed out the path which she must follow? Why was she sent to search for a child who was sheltered and safe?

There seemed to be a sort of mockery in this phantom guidance. She had been led to the very place where Jamie was to be found, only to be shown that he had no need of her at all. Every want of his was abundantly supplied; the fair lady had won his little heart; and the kiss which he vouchsafed to Elsie was merely bestowed at Mrs. Verdon's request. When Elsie released him he returned with alacrity to his adopted mother's side, and slid his hand into hers again.

Yet she had found him, and all suspense and anxiety were at an end. She thanked Mrs. Verdon for her courtesy, learned that Jamie's home was in Portman Square, and then gave her own address in return, and went quietly away with her two companions.

Arnold Wayne was left with Mrs. Verdon, who had recovered her courage, and was easily persuaded to re-enter her carriage. The horses had never bolted before; the coachman was not likely to fail in vigilance again; there was really no danger in taking the homeward drive. But she was a little nervous still, and it would be so very kind if Mr. Wayne would accompany her.

He was quite willing to accompany her.

It was a perfect summer evening, balmy and still; the air was full of delicate, dewy perfumes; a rich rose-colour burned in the west, and touched the silver gleam of the river with the last glow of the day. The carriage rolled easily along; Jamie, with sleepy blue eyes, half-open, enjoyed the motion in silent content. Mrs. Verdon, with gentle animation, talked to Mr. Wayne.

Elsie, walking slowly down the hill, caught a glimpse of the carriage and its occupants, and noted the dainty bonnet bending towards the dark head. A sense of loneliness, of aloofness, seemed to possess her that evening. The scent of flowers had something sad in its sweetness (as flower-scents often have); the sunset light suggested solemn thoughts. Mrs. Beaton remarked that she looked languid and pale.

"All this excitement has been too much for you, Miss Kilner," she said. "What a day we have had! How little we realised what was in store for us when we started this morning! But I shall sleep soundly to-night, knowing that Jamie is safe."

"It is a splendid thing for the boy," Elsie remarked. "What a beautiful child he is!"

"Yes; his beauty attracted Mrs. Verdon at first; but I think she loves him for his own sake. She is a charming lady, Miss Kilner."

"Very charming," Elsie admitted at once.

"And you'll go to see her, and tell us how Jamie goes on," Mrs. Beaton continued. "Mr. Wayne, too, will look after him; he won't lack friends."

"Supposing that Mrs. Verdon should marry again, what would she do with Jamie?" asked Mrs. Penn in a dismal voice. "Mr. Wayne seemed very attentive to her, I thought."

"It would be a very good thing for Jamie if she married Mr. Wayne, his uncle's old friend," Mrs. Beaton replied. "But I daresay she has a score of lovers. However, you may be sure that she will never neglect the boy."

"He's as haughty as a young lord," said Mrs. Penn. "Did you see how he tossed his head at me, and waved his hand to send me away?"

"Well, Mrs. Penn, he is a sensible child, and he remembers the treatment at Lee," answered Mrs. Beaton candidly. "We will let by-gones be bygones; but a child's memory keeps things shut up in it like a book. Andrew often astonished me when he was Jamie's age. He never would forget anything, especially if you wanted anything to be forgotten."

As the train sped homeward, Elsie looked from the window upon the shifting landscape, but observed nothing. All seemed a blank.

Her mind, so long intent on one object, was new deprived of its centre of thought. She recurred again and again to the old theme, only to say to herself a hundred times, "Jamie is safe." Had she lived so much upon this child that the secret of her interest had been self-forgetfulness? Her search was ended, and she was left alone — quite alone with herself.

She reached All Saints' Street between eight and nine o'clock. It was a clear night; the streets were full of carriages and people, and the lights of the lamps and shops had never been brighter. But an aspect of unreality pervaded everything, and she seemed to move through all these lights and sounds as if she were in a city of dreams.

When she had answered Miss Saxon's questions, and told her all that had happened in as few words as possible, she went upstairs to her sitting-room; and then she sank into a chair, leaning her head upon its back, and looking up at the stars above the roof.

Why was it that she was so melancholy to-night? She could have found it in her heart to have envied that fair woman who had gone away with the beautiful child by her side. Was Mrs. Verdon to have everything — wealth, position, Jamie's love, and — —

She sprang up suddenly from her chair in an agony of self-contempt and self-reproach. It is always a hard thing for a proud woman to learn the lesson of human weakness. Never before had Elsie suspected herself of anything so mean as jealousy. "Oh, Meta," she said, half-aloud, "your hand has pointed to a hard, lonely road, stretching out before me like a desert! Show me the rest—the home—that lies beyond the waste! It seems to-night as if, on earth or in heaven, there would never more be any home for me."

CHAPTER XI

MRS. VERDON

> "We know too much of Love ere we love. We can trace
> Nothing new, unexpected, or strange in his face
> When we see it at last. 'Tis the same little Cupid,
> With the same dimpled cheek and the smile almost stupid,
> We have seen in our pictures and stuck on our shelves,
> And copied, a hundred times over, ourselves."
>
> —Owen Meredith.

Mrs. Verdon held an untrammelled position in life. She was a rich young widow, uncontrolled, and without children. The death of her little boy had been a greater sorrow than the death of a husband who was much older than herself. Katherine Verdon had adored her child; it was Jamie's resemblance to her lost darling which had drawn her so strongly towards him. She had been a widow five years, and was in no haste to marry again. Like Queen Elizabeth, she coquetted with her suitors, but these coquetries were of a harmless kind, and never went far enough to set the world talking. She had a great deal of tact and cleverness, and managed all her affairs with graceful dexterity.

She was not really beautiful, but in a woman so fortunately situated a little beauty is made much of. Her figure, tall and slender, had the flexible grace of ribbon-grass; her little head, regally poised, was almost overweighted with thick braids of satiny hair of pale gold; small features, delicate, if irregular, a colourless, fair skin, and pale-blue eyes, completed this face, which never had a warm tint. Her dress was costly, but always well chosen, and she had so carefully studied herself that she could not put on anything which did not become her.

On that summer evening at Richmond she was at her best. Deliverance from great peril had opened her heart to all good influences. The fear of losing Jamie was set at rest, and it was a fear which had increased as the child grew dearer. She was genial, responsive, full of gentle gaiety and genuine gratitude.

For a whole year Arnold Wayne had listened to the praises of Katherine Verdon, chanted by his cousins the Danforths. They had found fault with him, as all his relations did, for leading an unsettled life, and were always asking when he was going to marry. He had been travelling for three or four years, associating with all sorts and conditions of men and women, interesting himself in strange religions, penetrating into regions which few Englishmen had ever visited, and he had reached the mature age of thirty-three without having been very deeply and seriously in love. Of course he had had love affairs. There was an Italian who had held him in her enchantments for a whole winter, not to mention a *gitàna*, whose liquid eyes had kept him spell-bound under the walls of the Alhambra, and others, fair and dark, tall and little, who had been—

> "The summer pilots of an empty heart
> Unto the shores of nothing."

But, as he had owned to his innermost self a hundred times, the woman who was to reign over his life had not yet come. Would she ever come? He had asked himself this question on the day when he had seen Elsie with the rector. Certainly, there had been a strange attraction in her face. It was beautiful, but he had seen beauties by the score; beauties of all lands and of all grades, high and low. It was not Elsie's beauty which had so strongly moved him, although it was of a type which he especially admired. It was an expression— a something that was wistful and tender in the eyes—a look as of one who was waiting before the fast-shut door of paradise. In time the face might have passed out of his memory, but it flashed upon him again at Richmond, and he had a prophetic feeling that his fate had come to him at last.

The boy Jamie, as he saw at once, would be the connecting-link between Elsie and himself. It would be perfectly right in him to call on one who had taken so warm an interest in the nephew of his intimate friend.

Then, too, there had been something said about Miss Neale's manuscript, in which his name was mentioned. He felt that he ought to examine the manuscript, and carry out, as far as he could, the wishes of the writer.

These were the thoughts which came crowding into his mind during the drive home from Richmond. Meanwhile Mrs. Verdon was talking to him in silvery tones, and asking, with pleasant friendliness, whether he had made any plans for the autumn. Jamie, rosy and sleepy, gave him an indolent smile now and then. It was a curious thing, he reflected, that the child should link him to Mrs. Verdon as well as to Miss Kilner. And then he smiled to himself, remembering all that the Danforths had said in this fair widow's praise. Her carriage set him down in a convenient spot, and he walked away to his chambers in Piccadilly, pondering over the strange adventures of the day.

Mrs. Verdon, although she loved liberty, was not unprotected, and her late husband's sister—a Mrs. Tell—had lived with her all through the years of her widowhood. Mrs. Tell, too, was a rich widow, tall, and of imposing aspect, but easy-tempered and rather lazy. She was past sixty, and looked a majestic matron, with her white hair and lace cap. Katherine's whims did not annoy her in the least, and she had taken quite kindly to Jamie. In her inmost heart she did not want her sister-in-law to marry again, and the boy, she thought, would fill up the void in her life, and help to make her contented with her lot.

Mrs. Verdon had a good deal of pleasure in her large house. She found her pictures, chairs, tables, plaques, and hangings quite absorbing sometimes. Many a morning was spent in arranging and rearranging cabinets and mantels, and trying the effect of new draperies; and Mrs. Tell enjoyed anything that made the time pass tranquilly away.

The carriage stopped at the door in Portman Square. Sleepy Jamie went toiling up the wide staircase in the dusk, and Mrs. Verdon slowly followed. Everything looked rich and dim; the plants in the great Indian jars filled the hall with sweet scents. Flowers were blooming in every nook. Through a half-drawn *portière* there was a glimpse of Mrs. Tell reading in the shaded lamplight.

A motherly woman met Jamie on the landing, and gave him a loving greeting. She had been nurse to Mrs. Verdon's own child.

"Ready for bed?" she said in her cheery voice. "What pretty dreams you'll have to-night!"

"Horses ran away," Jamie began, opening his blue eyes. "Went faster than my rocking-horse! Dreadful! Don't want to go out in the carriage any more."

"Never mind," said nurse, with a little hug, "we won't talk about runaway horses at bedtime. We'll just shut our eyes and think of a field of yellow corn, waving, waving, waving."

Elsie had often been troubled with sad visions of Jamie at night. She had pictured him sleeping in rags under an arch, or in some corner of a grimy garret. But fancy had never shown her anything like the dainty little white bed in this spacious room.

Gaily-coloured prints decorated the walls, and on a bracket just above the boy's pillow stood a lovely statuette of an angel, with folded wings and down-bent gracious face. When any visitor came up to see the night-nursery, Jamie would point at once to the figure and say proudly, "My guardian angel."

An hour or two later, when Jamie, rosy and beautiful, was wrapped in the deep sweet sleep of childhood, Mrs. Verdon and her sister-in-law were sitting together after dinner.

"What an eventful day you have had!" said Mrs. Tell, looking up from her knitting in the softly-shaded light. "And what a romantic meeting with Mr. Wayne! Is he all that the Danforths described?"

"Of course not," replied Mrs. Verdon. "They described one of the impossible heroes of fiction. You know, they have a talent for description."

"But isn't he nice?" Mrs. Tell asked.

"Yes, he is nice. There is something about him that is not commonplace."

She leaned back in her chair with a half-smile, absently toying with a sprig of lemon-plant. Her slender figure looked graceful in a gown of some soft kind of silk, flowered with faint blue and pink.

Looking at her, you somehow imbibed the notion that her hair, eyes, complexion, and dress corresponded with her character. She was faintly coloured. Nothing about her was intense.

A vague thought of this kind flitted through Mrs. Tell's brain at this moment. She was not a clever woman, but long intercourse with the world had quickened her faculty for observation, and she was much given to studying Katherine.

"Not commonplace," she repeated; "then, of course, you found him very interesting?"

"There was not time to get interested in him," Mrs. Verdon answered.

"Naturally if a man saves one's life one feels grateful. Perhaps my gratitude has invested him with a fictitious charm."

She spoke with a little mocking air, twisting the sprig of lemon-plant in her long white fingers, and looking down meditatively at the carpet.

"He will follow up his advantage," remarked Mrs. Tell, knitting steadily. "No man ever had a more favourable introduction. I wonder if he knew whose carriage it was when he stopped the horses? It was very well done. Of course, a man who has travelled for years, and gone into all sorts of risky places, is always ready for an emergency. He will call soon."

"He will call soon," echoed the younger widow, still with the little touch of mockery in her tone, "and I shall ask him to dinner. And then, Olivia, you will sit there in your pet chair and watch us both over your knitting-pins. When men come here, you always remind me of Madame Defarge and the dreadful knitting-women of the French Revolution. You have knitted all my admirers into that coverlet you are making. It's a sort of secret record, I do believe."

She rose, with a slight laugh, suppressed a yawn in saying goodnight, and went out of the room with a soft rustle of trailing draperies, leaving Mrs. Tell sitting in the "pet-chair."

CHAPTER XII

HIS FIRST VISIT

> "The roses bloom while the lady waits,
> The lark sings high in the blue above;
> But who will open the golden gates,
> And let her in to the realms of love?"

Arnold Wayne's first call upon Elsie was always a very distinct memory to him afterwards. People were beginning to go out of town, and those who remained were haunted by the thought of breezy uplands, or of a blue summer sea breaking lazily on the golden sands. As Arnold walked along All Saints' Street, about five in the afternoon, the chime of a bell ringing for evensong reminded him of his old home at Rushbrook and the grey church close to his gates.

So it came to pass that he went into Elsie's presence haunted by memories of his boyhood, and there was nothing in her presence to dispel such memories; something about her seemed to blend with them and harmonise with early associations.

She had been sitting by the open window with a book upon her lap, and she rose to meet him, still holding the volume in her hand. She was dressed in a pale-grey gown, and wore a large bunch of heliotrope in the folds of a kerchief of soft muslin knotted at her breast. The quiet little room was flooded with sunshine; the bell kept up its chime; some white pigeons went flying past the window.

"You have made a home here," he said involuntarily; and then he thought of those wise words of Ruskin's: "Wherever a true wife comes, this home is always round her. The stars only may be over her head, the glow-worm in the night-cold grass may be the only fire at her foot; but home is yet wherever she is."

"Yes," she answered quietly, "it is a safe nook, where I can be at peace."

"She has known storms, then," was Arnold's mental comment.

He began to speak of Jamie, and a light came suddenly into her face. It was the greatest relief, she said, to know that the child was happy.

"And Miss Neale's manuscript—may I see it?" he asked. "I have always wished that I had known her. When Waring wrote to tell me of his engagement I was abroad. The letter followed me from place to place."

"The manuscript was discovered by chance. I keep it where I first found it," said Elsie, going to the old table in the corner. She took the roll of paper out of the drawer and put it into his hand. There was perfect silence in the room while he turned over the pages. Elsie had gone back to her window-seat and sat there motionless.

"If they were with us now the world would be all the better for them," he said, looking up at last. "I would give a great deal to grasp Waring's hand again. And Meta—it was best for her to follow him."

"Yes," Elsie answered; "it was best. I am glad, and yet I often wish she was here."

"You have loved these two without seeing them?" he said, looking at her intently.

"It is easy," she returned, "to know men and women by the footprints they have left and the harvest which they have sown. There are those whom, having not seen, we love."

A shade came over his face. "If I were to die," he said suddenly, "no one would ever love me for the sake of what I had left. As to footprints, they would soon be effaced; and as to the harvest, nothing would crop up but a few wild oats. It's rather a depressing thought, isn't it?"

"Yes," she answered, looking at him in her turn. He was conscious that her soft, dark eyes were resting on him very thoughtfully, and that they were full of gentleness.

He had been left an orphan at nineteen, but he had never blamed any one but himself for the fact that he had done nothing in his life, and that he was going on doing nothing. Uncle Harry Danforth, his mother's brother, had looked after the Rushbrook estate for years, and had spared Arnold all possible trouble. He had given up all responsibilities, just because he chose to give up and let himself drift. But there are moments when a man wakes up to a sudden consciousness that he has trifled with himself and his past. Had he come here to meet the touch of the vanished hand? There was a pause, and again the soft white wings flew past the window. Then Elsie spoke in a very quiet voice.

"I suppose," she said, "that there are a good many miles before you yet. You might try a new path and begin sowing afresh."

It was a simple speech, uttered in the simplest manner possible, but it came to him like a new truth. Yet it was a very old thing that she had said—a thing that others had spoken to him a hundred times at least, and he had been as deaf as a stone. Most of the ideas that have really stirred our hearts owe their power to the voice that speaks them.

"Thirty-three is rather an advanced age for a man to begin sowing," he answered. "But I might try, if you think it worth while."

She smiled, a sweet smile that crept up from her lips into her eyes, and lingered there.

"I think it is worth while," she said.

"Very well; I had better start at Rushbrook in the literal sense. My uncle will be delighted, although the ground has been thoroughly looked after, I believe. My relations have done their utmost to make an agriculturist of me. If I spend an autumn down there, and take an interest in things, it will be regarded as a hopeful sign."

"Then you have a home in the country," said Elsie, with a little sigh.

The sigh was not lost on Arnold.

"Yes, I have a quaint old place in Blankshire," he replied. "It overlooks a valley of many streams, in the midst of a quiet pastoral country. Can I persuade you to come and see it with the Lennards, Miss Kilner? Most people think it rather pleasant."

"The Lennards? Oh, I fancy they are going to Switzerland," she said. "I am not sure about their plans, and I have not made any arrangements yet."

"I shall write to Mr. Lennard to-night," Arnold remarked. "If I'm to begin to make myself useful I shall expect all my friends to come to my aid. May I count upon your help, Miss Kilner?"

There was an undertone of earnestness in the light speech and a look of eagerness in his face.

"I would help if I could," she answered. "As to the country, I see it always in my dreams. It is a lost Paradise to me."

"Then why did you leave it?" he asked suddenly.

She coloured, and the dark lashes veiled the trouble in her eyes.

His heart ached for her. Yet, being human, all sorts of doubts and fears came crowding into his brain. Was there an old love-affair and undying constancy? With that intense face of hers she could hardly have escaped love's sorrows.

And then, in an instant, came a flash of wonder at himself. Was he already so nearly in love that he dreaded a possible rival?

"Circumstances were too strong for me," she replied. "The rector and Mrs. Lennard knew that I had to go. I came to London because I have more friends here than anywhere else."

There was a tremor in her voice that touched him. He felt a sudden longing to be her champion, and prove that "circumstances" were not too strong for him. A man never looks so well as when he is under the influence of a chivalrous feeling; it can transfigure even a dull face, and Arnold's face was anything but dull. Poor Elsie happened to glance at him at that moment, and a soft glow flushed her cheeks. She tried hard not to think that she was losing her heart.

"It would be so dreadful," she thought, "if I were to make a fool of myself at nine-and-twenty! Can't I venture to enjoy a little friendliness without getting hot cheeks like a school-girl?"

After he was gone she sat dreaming till it grew dusk, and wondering what would become of her when Arnold Wayne had married Mrs. Verdon.

The pigeons had gone to roost, the last blush of crimson had faded from the sky, and the first stars were twinkling faintly in the gloaming. Elsie thought of Meta, lifted out of all the doubts and troubles of this poor life, and envied her perfect peace.

"Ah," she sighed, "if I could only see her home for one moment, how bravely I could go on living here!"

CHAPTER XIII

IN PORTMAN SQUARE

> "And quite alone I never felt,
> I knew that Thou wert near,
> A silence tingling in the room,
> A strangely pleasant fear."
>
> —Faber.

Arnold Wayne took his way to Portman Square, thinking about Elsie as he went along. If those two could have looked into each other's hearts just then, they would speedily have come to an understanding.

When he went up the steps of the great house and entered the flower-scented hall, he was in a dreamy mood. And when he found himself in Mrs. Verdon's artistically furnished drawing-room, he had a queer notion that only his phantom self was here and his real self had remained in the little room in All Saints' Street.

His hostess looked very slender and tall and fair in her mauve silk dress. Her satiny hair, wound round her small head, conveyed the idea that if unbound it would enshroud her, like Lady Godiva's, in a veil. The rich glowing colours of the furniture and hangings formed themselves into a harmonious background for the graceful figure.

Mrs. Tell was quietly observing the new-comer, and silently deciding that the chances were in his favour. She had not the faintest doubt about his intentions. All the men who came here proposed to her sister-in-law, and of course he would do the same.

Everybody allowed that nothing could be more agreeable than Mrs. Verdon's position and surroundings. The house exactly suited Mrs. Tell. Katherine, whom she liked in her cool way, was not difficult to live with; any change was to be dreaded. But there was always the fear that change would come, and she had an instinctive dread of this Mr. Wayne.

"And so you have been calling on Miss Kilner?" said Mrs. Verdon, as they sat at dinner. "She must come and see me and Jamie. Has she many friends?"

"A great many," replied Arnold, who did not know anything about them.

"I daresay I have met her somewhere," Mrs. Verdon went on. "I have either met her or seen her face in a picture. She has quite a picture-face, hasn't she?"

"Ah, perhaps she has," said Wayne abstractedly, as if the idea had been presented to him for the first time.

"I must have seen her in a picture." Mrs. Tell noticed that Katherine seemed bent on keeping to the subject. "There is a painting of a young woman clasping a Bible to her breast. Don't you know it? That is like her, I think."

"Ah, very likely," rejoined Arnold in an expressionless voice. "I know a man who is always painting pictures of that kind. His girls are always going to suffer for their faith, and they have many costumes, but only one face. It becomes monotonous."

Mrs. Verdon laughed.

"I had my portrait painted once," she said, "but it wasn't like me — it was too intense. I couldn't look like that unless my whole nature had changed. I don't like strong feelings, they make life so uncomfortable."

"Very uncomfortable," assented Mrs. Tell in a lazy voice. "And, besides, they are undignified. You are always so deliciously calm, Katherine, that you make people fall in love with repose."

"This house would be a home for the lotus-eaters," said Mrs. Verdon. "I love perfumes and stillness and subdued light. Jamie exercises his lungs and legs in the top rooms, but he seldom breaks the tranquillity that reigns downstairs."

When they sat in the drawing-room after dinner, Arnold mentally decided that it was very easy to fall in love with repose—for a little while.

Katherine talked to him in her silvery tones, looking at him now and then with her pretty, faint smile. The folds of the delicate mauve gown trailed over the rich carpet. She leant lazily back in her chair, waving a plumy fan, sometimes, with a soft, even motion.

The doors of the conservatory were open; light curtains were looped back, giving glimpses of a mass of blossoms; the atmosphere was laden with perfumes. Yes, it was all very pleasant—for a little while.

Arnold Wayne did not try to persuade himself that he should enjoy it always. His was not the temperament of the lotus-eater. His nature craved a rich, warm life, full of strong light and shade. Still, he was glad when Mrs. Verdon told him that she should start for Rushbrook in a fortnight.

"I have taken The Cedars again," she said. "The air agreed with Jamie and me last year. We both want to be freshened up. It will be nice to be near the Danforths; I get on with them so well."

"They are always talking about you," rejoined Arnold, with perfect truth.

When he was gone, the two widows sat in silence for a little while. The elder knitted diligently; the younger toyed with her feathery fan.

"What do you think of him, Olivia?" Mrs. Verdon asked at last. There was a faint ring of impatience in her tone. She had been waiting for the other to speak first.

"There is something uncommon in him which makes him attractive," replied Mrs. Tell, without glancing up from her work. "And he doesn't seem anxious to attract. Not that he is indifferent, but— —"

"Of course he is not indifferent." Katherine's silvery voice was shriller than usual. "I found it very easy to please him. But he is not a gushing man. I hate gushing men."

"So do I," returned Mrs. Tell. "No, he is not gushing; but I think— yes, I am sure—that he could be emotional if he were to let himself go."

"Really, Olivia, I didn't give you credit for so much imagination," said Mrs. Verdon sharply. "Now, I am quite sure that he would never, under any circumstances, be emotional. He has travelled a great deal and seen everything, and he is just in the state to enjoy repose. He would like even to glide quietly into love without disturbing his calmness."

Then, prompted by an utterly unaccountable impulse, Mrs. Tell made one of the greatest mistakes she had ever made in her life. "Do you know, Katherine," she said, "I think you have at last found a man who doesn't mean to propose to you?"

Mrs. Verdon's fan ceased its regular come-and-go and lay motionless in her lap. She did not speak, and Mrs. Tell, who had expected her to laugh at her little speech, was startled by her silence. Presently Katherine rose, with a sort of queenliness which became her very well. "I am tired to-night," she said, quite ignoring her sister-in-law's remark. "In this hot weather one begins to pine for the country. Jamie has looked pale to-day. By-the-way, I shall call on Miss Kilner to-morrow, and ask her to dinner before we go away." Then she went off to her room without another word, and Mrs. Tell was left alone with the consciousness of her blunder.

If Katherine was tired, her eyes had never been more wakeful. Her maid, who entered noiselessly, found her standing by a window overlooking the garden, gazing out into the moonlight. It was a

London garden, dry and dusty by day, but at night, when the trees were touched by the mysterious light, it had an aspect of romance.

In silence she sat before the glass, while Bennet's dexterous fingers unbraided the silky hair and brushed it before coiling it up for the night. Looking at the face reflected in the glass, she perceived that it was not quite so tranquil as usual, and was irritated at finding that Mrs. Tell's words had disturbed her. Why was she disturbed? Her vanity had taken a chill, that was all.

"I am vainer than I thought myself," she mused. "All women are vain, of course. It is not a very bad fault, but it makes one little in one's own sight." Then came other ideas, crowding fast into her brain. "What does Olivia know? She is not a clever woman. How can she tell what a man means to do? Away down there in Rushbrook he will be put to the test. I am always at my best in the country; the air freshens me, and the quietness rests me. And my dresses are lovely — on that ground I stand alone."

Yet, in spite of this comforting conclusion, Katherine was restless under Bennet's hands, and glad to be left in solitude.

On the following afternoon, Elsie, dreaming over her solitary cup and saucer, was startled when her parlour door opened. Mrs. Verdon, bland and smiling, came in, followed by Jamie. The boy lifted his blue eyes solemnly to Elsie's face, and something he saw there curved his lips into a smile and brought a dimple into his beautiful cheeks. As usual, he wore his sailor-suit, and this time he accepted Elsie's kiss with perfect graciousness.

"We must know each other better," said Mrs. Verdon, really touched by Elsie's feeling for the child. She talked on, pleasantly and fluently. It was evidently her fancy to make much of Miss Kilner and take possession of her.

Elsie accepted the invitation to dinner, partly because Mrs. Verdon was really a very pleasant person, but chiefly because her heart still clung to Jamie. On her arrival she was taken up to the top of the great house, and shown the two spacious rooms which were his own.

"I does as I like up here," said Jamie grandly (grammar was occasionally forgotten). "Mammy never 'feres with me." Elsie followed him when he led the way through the door which opened into the night nursery. The first object which attracted her gaze was the statuette on the bracket over the bed. Jamie at once introduced the figure as his guardian angel. "I am never afraid at nights," the little fellow said. "Some boys is. The angel never goes to sleep; he's always awake up there. If anything wicked came, he'd just make himself large and spread his wings right over me."

Jamie spoke with an air of perfect confidence which went to Elsie's heart, and her thoughts found mental expression in Browning's beautiful words:—

> "Dear and great angel, wouldst thou only leave
> That child, when thou hast done with him, for me!"

Poor lonely Elsie! She, too, desired to feel the soft, white wings close round her, shutting out all miseries of trouble and doubt, and enfolding her in their healing atmosphere of peace.

CHAPTER XIV

RUSHBROOK

> "About the windings of the maze to hear
> The soft wind blowing. Over meadowy holms
> And alders, garden aisles."
>
> —Tennyson.

Arnold Wayne wrote his letter to Mr. Lennard, but the rector had already made arrangements to go to Switzerland. Mrs. Lennard, however, had decided not to accompany him; she had made up her mind to spend a couple of months with a maiden lady living at Rushbrook, and it was her wish that Elsie Kilner should be with her there. So it came to pass that Jamie and the three people who were linked together through his little person all came to sojourn within a stone's-throw of each other. Miss Ryan and Mrs. Lennard had been school-fellows and bosom friends, and the friendship had lasted through all the chances and changes of life.

Willow Farm and its broad acres belonged to Miss Ryan, and was managed for her by her nephew Francis. She lived in an old-fashioned house, long and low, with quaint dormer-windows set in a peaked roof of red tiles. The house stood in the middle of a garden filled to overflowing with country flowers, and the warm, sweet perfume of the crowded beds made Elsie feel that she had come close to the very heart of summer. The sun was ripening the black, juicy berries on the loaded cherry-trees; bees kept up a ceaseless hum; large roses pressed close together in masses of bloom.

"What a little world of sweets!" said Elsie, smelling a bunch of crimson carnations.

She was standing on the door-step after breakfast, wearing her pretty grey gown, and a creamy muslin kerchief knotted at the throat. Her face, under the golden straw-hat, was so richly, yet delicately, coloured that it wore the aspect of a flower.

A slim, tall man, of eight or nine and twenty, stood looking at that face in the morning light; he had just given her the carnations. "I am glad you like the old place here," he said. "It isn't as romantic, of course, as Wayne's Court, but it is comfortable. You know Wayne? He is a very good fellow."

"I met him in town," Elsie answered.

"Ah, yes! he knows your friends the Lennards. What a wanderer he has been! But now, they tell me, he seems inclined to settle down at last."

"That is a good thing," said Elsie, raising the carnations to her face.

"He'll marry, I suppose," Francis Ryan went on. "The Danforths are trying to make up the match with Mrs. Verdon. Do you know her? A fair woman, with sky-blue eyes. She has come to The Cedars again, close to the Court; so that looks as if she meant business."

This was the news that Elsie heard on her first day at Willow Farm. It gave her a strong desire for solitude, and she was glad

when Francis said that he must go and look after one of the horses.
She waited until he had disappeared, and then went down a long
gravelled walk, between crowded borders, to a little white gate.
Lifting the latch, she walked across a green meadow, and found
herself close to the brink of a river. Rushbrook was a place of many
waters, a land of green and silver, beautiful with the peace that
belongs to a pastoral country. She soon found a cosy nook on an old
tree-trunk in the shade, and sat down to think. It was a good spot
for a reverie. You could listen to the whisper of the water among the
sedges, and look off, across the river, to the low-lying meadows
beyond—a scene which was fascinating in its intense quietness. It
rests the eye and brain to gaze at those cool green levels, broidered
with silvery rivulets, and watch the water stealing among rushes
and tall rustling reeds.

"IT WAS A GOOD SPOT FOR A REVERIE."

It was a lovely morning—soft, hazy, exquisite, as mornings in August often are. Looking back across the meadow, Elsie saw a row of copper-beeches standing in an even line against the deep, dreamy blue of the sky. Away to the left was a mass of foliage hiding the red peaked roof of Willow Farm.

She had not expected to be very happy when she came to Rushbrook. Deep down in her heart was a fear which she kept carefully covered over; she was ashamed of its very existence, and strove to hide it from her own sight. It was Mrs. Verdon—always Mrs. Verdon—who was to have everything worth having.

Of course, it was the most natural thing in the world that Mr. Wayne should fall in love with Mrs. Verdon. The match would be approved by everybody, and Elsie's judgment just then was not clear enough to see that the matches approved by everybody are precisely those which seldom take place.

It was jealousy—ugly, plain, unconquerable jealousy—which was tormenting Elsie now. It is a dreadful moment when a woman looks deep into her innermost self and catches the gleam of a fierce fire burning there.

She looked out again at the shining water, and drew in deep breaths of pure air. The freshness of the streams was in the atmosphere; all around was the intense greenness of water-fed grass.

What a sweet old earth it was, after all! Green pastures and still waters were to be found by all who let the angels guide them. It is our own fault always if we enter the barren and dry land where no water is.

The old trunk on which she sat was close to the edge of the water. Overhead the spreading boughs of an elm protected her from the sun; a little bird, hidden among the leaves, gave out a clear note now and then. Elsie, feeling a sense of comfort stealing into her heart unawares, began to listen to the bird. The bunch of carnations lay upon her knee.

A rustling in the grasses near made her start. Arnold Wayne was coming down the slope of the bank to the spot where she was sitting.

"What a charming nook you have discovered!" he said, his brown face lighting up with pleasure at the sight of her. "I have been to Willow Farm to seek you."

"How did you know that I was here?" Elsie asked as she gave him her hand.

"Mrs. Lennard was standing at a window upstairs when you went out. She watched you cross the field and go down to the river. I heard that you arrived last night."

"Yes," said Elsie, a contented look coming into her brown eyes. "It is delicious to get away from London, delicious to tread on cool grass instead of hot paving-stones."

"And you are going to stay in Rushbrook a long time. Mrs. Lennard has been telling me all her plans. The rector is coming here on his return from Switzerland, and then you will all pay the long-promised visit to the Court."

"We shall see," Elsie returned, with a little air of gravity. "The present is so lovely that I don't care to look into the future, Mr. Wayne. I am charmed with the river. I like to smell the damp, fresh scent of the sedges."

"I'm glad it does you good," he answered, rather absently. "You have some fine carnations there," he added, lightly touching the flowers on her lap.

"Yes; Mr. Ryan gathered them after breakfast."

She spoke the words without thinking about them at all, and she was not looking at Arnold when she uttered them. If his face changed, she did not see it.

"So he is beginning to give her flowers already," Arnold thought.

Meanwhile Elsie was wondering whether he had yet seen Mrs. Verdon. The two widows had travelled down to Rushbrook on Monday, and this was Wednesday.

"Jamie must be delighted to be here," she said after a little pause.

"He is quite radiant," Arnold replied. "What lungs the boy has! I could hear him shouting as I walked up the lane to The Cedars yesterday afternoon."

"So he has called on her already," Elsie thought.

"Mrs. Verdon is afraid of the river," he went on. "The young rascal wants to make straight for the water; he has brought a regular fleet with him. They will have to keep a sharp watch."

"He is a dear little man," Elsie said warmly. "If your friend had lived he would have been proud of his nephew."

"I hope he'll grow up as good as dear old Harold," rejoined Arnold in a graver tone. "And I hope, too, that he won't miss Harold's influence over his life. He's in a fair way to be spoilt, you see."

"Mrs. Verdon really wants to do her best for him," said Elsie, with perfect sincerity. "And nurse is a very sensible woman."

"But it takes a man to manage a strong boy. A woman can't do it alone."

"He will help her to manage him," Elsie thought. "It is right, I know. This is what Meta would have wished. I am beginning to hate myself."

Aloud she said pleasantly, "I shall call at The Cedars to-morrow, and say that I will take care of Jamie sometimes."

"I came to ask you all to dine at the Court on Saturday," said Arnold, after another brief silence. "Mrs. Lennard will come, and so will Ryan; but Miss Ryan declined. I want you to get acquainted with my old place, Miss Kilner; there are one or two pictures which you will like, I think."

"Thank you," Elsie answered frankly. "I am very fond of pictures."

"You were looking at a picture when I saw you first," Arnold Wayne remarked, gazing at her with remembering eyes. "You were quite absorbed in it, and saw nothing else. And you only came out of your dream when the rector shouted a greeting to me."

Elsie smiled, and there was something dreamy in the smile. She had changed her attitude as she sat on the old trunk, and had laid the carnations on the bark by her side.

"I remember the picture," she said in a musing tone. "Two nuns were waiting outside a convent door. One of these days I think I shall be a nun."

"No, you won't," he answered in a masterful voice. "Will you walk a little way along the bank? There's a picturesque island farther on, a wonderful place for wild-flowers."

She rose. And the bunch of carnations was left forgotten on the trunk of the tree.

CHAPTER XV

WAYNE'S COURT

> "Love in my bosom, like a bee,
> Doth suck his sweet;
> Now with his wings he plays with me,
> Now with his feet."

> —Rosalind's Madrigal.

Mrs. Lennard was a pleasant old lady, with a sunny temper and a strong will. She always had her own way, and decided all doubtful matters with a charming imperiousness which offended nobody.

Elsie had been accustomed to look up to the rector's wife from her earliest days. To the rectory she had always carried her burdens and secret sorrows, and Mrs. Lennard's sympathy had sweetened many bitter hours.

The golden light was streaming into Elsie's room as she stood before the glass, dressing for the dinner-party at the Court. It was a quaint room, with a chest-of-drawers of Queen Anne's time, and slender-legged tables and chairs, black with age, and Elsie, in a soft, trailing gown of cream-coloured silk, looked almost too modern for her surroundings.

After that stroll by the river on Wednesday morning she had schooled herself to take life in a calm fashion.

On Thursday she had called at The Cedars, and had been received with the utmost cordiality. Jamie had seized upon her with the freedom of long acquaintance, insisting that she should inspect the stock of toys he had brought from London. As a mark of special favour he dropped a tin soldier into her cup of tea, and presented her with a loathly green lizard out of his Noah's Ark.

On Friday he came to Willow Farm and gladdened the hearts of the two old ladies. Francis Ryan's enjoyment was less noticeable; he found the little fellow a decided bore. There was not a single quiet minute with Miss Kilner; she was devoted to the boy, and would not let him go out of her sight. Arnold Wayne, who dropped in unexpectedly, behaved in quite a fatherly manner to Jamie, and did not hesitate to rebuke him when his gambols went too far.

Looking back on the past four days, Elsie acknowledged to herself that they had been days of pleasantness. Once, Francis had openly remarked that he wondered how soon Mrs. Verdon and Wayne would come to an understanding; and Mrs. Lennard had replied that it was only the unexpected that ever came to pass.

The dear old lady, in her black silk dress and Honiton lace cap, came rustling softly into the room on this golden evening.

"Elsie," she said, "you are to wear my flowers. Mr. Ryan is cutting some in the greenhouse at this moment, but I am before him. Gloire de Dijon roses and scarlet geranium set in maidenhair! Isn't that a lovely spray? Your old friend knows what will become you best!"

"Of course she does," responded Elsie, with a kiss. "They are perfectly beautiful flowers, and no one else could have arranged them so well. Flowers suit me ever so much better than jewels, Mrs. Lennard."

"Yes, my dear. But where are your mother's diamonds?"

"I have not got them," Elsie answered quietly. "I saw Bertha wearing them just before my father died. Don't be vexed, dearest Mrs. Lennard."

But the old lady was vexed; a flush mounted to the roots of her silver hair, and her foot beat upon the carpet.

"Then I suppose some of Robert's creditors have got them now," she said angrily. "Bertha deserves all that she has had to bear. It is just chastisement. I wonder that you can take your wrongs so patiently!"

Elsie turned to her gently, with a wonderfully sweet look in her brown eyes.

"I was not patient at first," she answered. "There was a battle to fight. Afterwards, Meta helped me."

"Meta?" repeated Mrs. Lennard in a puzzled tone. "Ah, you mean the lady who was engaged to Harold Waring. How did she help you, my dear?"

"I think it was the touch of her vanished hand that calmed me," Elsie said in a hushed tone. "Like Hamlet, 'I am very proud, revengeful, ambitious;' I was glad at first when I heard of Bertha's humiliation. And then I read Meta's story in her manuscript, and knew that she had suffered more than I, and had forgiven."

She stood quite still a moment, a graceful figure enfolded in golden light, with an exalted look on her face.

"Elsie," Mrs. Lennard said suddenly, "you are a beautiful woman. You are like some one in a poem, child! There is a certain kind of beauty that only comes through pain."

Elsie smiled at her, and began to fasten the flowers in her bodice. They gave the finishing touch to her dress, and suited her, as she had said, better than jewels.

There was an ancient bridge across the moat which divided the Court from the highway. The water lay still and shining under the broad lily leaves, and the grey walls of the old house stood bathed in the enchanted light. It was an evening that made you think of legend and song, of knights riding home across the bridge when the fight was over, of ladies watching from those windows high for the first glimpse of streaming pennon and waving plume.

The old house stood fair and stately in the sunset, with all its oriel windows and pointed gables and gilded vanes. As Elsie went up the grey stone steps of the terrace she had that curious feeling which Rossetti has called "sudden light"—

"I have been here before,
But when or how I cannot tell."

Nothing seemed unfamiliar; the dense walls of box and yew showing dark against a saffron sky, the half-defaced knightly figure above the great portico, the tiled floor of the hall, where a few white rose-petals were scattered.

A little later, when she sat down with the other guests to dine in a long room, dark with much black carved oak, she still had the dreamy sensation of returning to a life forgotten. The guests, however, were strangers. Mrs. Verdon, in a white silk gown embroidered with bunches of poppies, had never seemed less known. The grey-headed man with the rosy face was Mr. Danforth, and the two auburn-haired young ladies were his daughters, Mary and Lily.

Before that evening was over it occurred to Elsie that one or two persons were made slightly uncomfortable by her presence at the Court; and one of them, Lily Danforth, showed her uneasiness rather plainly.

She was a pretty girl, who owed her prettiness chiefly to her bright colouring and the freshness of youth. Her white dress, relieved only by touches of the palest green, became her very well. But she was restless, and Elsie saw that her eyes often glanced quickly and furtively in the direction of Francis Ryan.

All the Danforths treated Elsie rather distantly, but they were devoted to Mrs. Verdon. As there was no mistress of Wayne's Court, it fell to Mary's part to play hostess, and when she gave the signal to rise from the table Elsie felt that she was going into a chilly atmosphere.

In a hundred little ways did Miss Danforth contrive to slight Miss Kilner. Mary had never been as pretty as Lily, and was ten or twelve years older. It was not unknown to family friends that, after hoping vainly to win Arnold Wayne for herself, she was now trying hard to provide him with a wife of her own choosing.

But there was one person who was more than a match for Miss Danforth, and that was Mrs. Lennard. The old lady was not ignorant of her devices; her own knowledge of the world was far greater than Mary could ever hope to attain. The rector's wife had been a society belle in her youth, and had not forgotten the use of her weapons. Mary was discomfited, and Mrs. Verdon and Mrs. Tell were immensely amused when Mrs. Lennard proved herself mistress of the situation.

The drawing-room had the look of a room that is seldom inhabited; the keys of the piano were stiff through lack of use. It was so warm that the windows (which were modern in this part of the house) had been widely opened, and the scent of flowers drifted in from the terrace. Arnold, entering with the other men, detected Elsie sitting in the shade of a lace curtain and looking out into the golden moonlight.

He was at her side in a moment. Francis Ryan, who had searched for her in a wrong direction, saw that he had lost his chance, and went over to talk to Mrs. Verdon.

"Come out and see how the streams glisten in the moonlight," said Arnold in a quiet voice. And Elsie consented willingly; she was tired of the formal room and the uninteresting talk, and the breath of the night was sweet.

The ground sloped gently down from the terrace, and beyond the Court gardens were the low-lying meadows and shining watercourses. The glamour of the moonshine was over all; it was like a landscape seen in a dream.

"I must see more of you next week," said Arnold, looking down at the delicate face which was spiritualised by the mysterious light. "You will come to church to-morrow. There will be a walk of three-quarters of a mile; the footpath runs through the fields."

"It will be delightful to go to a country church again," Elsie answered.

"I'm glad to return to the old rural scenes myself," Arnold confessed. "By the way, don't turn poor Ryan's head, Miss Kilner, unless you want to break some one's heart."

"Whose heart?"

Elsie looked up at him with grave, questioning eyes.

"My cousin Lily's. It's quite an old affair."

"Oh, yes, we'll all go out on the terrace. No, Mrs. Tell, we shan't take cold. It can't be done to-night."

Mary Danforth was speaking; her high-pitched voice grated unpleasantly on Elsie's ears. She stepped out over the low window-sill, followed by Mrs. Verdon, Lily, and Mr. Ryan.

Arnold muttered something under his breath. Mary came towards the pair at once, with a little affected exclamation of surprise.

"You here, Arnold! Isn't it lovely, Miss Kilner? The view from the terrace is always so pretty by moonlight. How very warm it is! But don't you think you ought to have a shawl?"

They were all mixed up now; there were no more quiet words. Everybody seemed to talk and laugh at once.

A stable-clock struck ten, and Mrs. Lennard told Elsie that it was time to go.

Francis Ryan and his two ladies went back across the old bridge. Miss Kilner, wrapt in a soft buff shawl, paused a second to look down into the dark moat. Only a few moonbeams touched the still water; the rushes stood up like tall black spears; one could fancy armed men crouched in ambush there in the shadow of the arch. She walked on again by Mrs. Lennard's side.

"We were rather dull at the Court to-night," said Francis. "Wayne has grown accustomed to living in tents, and that sort of thing, you see. The old place needs a lady's rule. Mrs. Verdon will make a good *chatelaine*."

"Has she been telling you her secrets?" Mrs. Lennard asked.

"No; but the Danforths were talking."

"The Danforths generally are talking," the old lady replied.

"Well, but I think they are right. It's time for Wayne to settle. A man should look after his own place and know his own people. And if he has a big house he wants a wife."

"When he wants her he can find her without the assistance of other people. The worst matches I've ever known were those made up by sisters and cousins and aunts," said Mrs. Lennard in her decided way. "Elsie, my dear, what are you looking at? That was only a cat that ran across the road. You are getting nervous. I shall send you off to bed."

CHAPTER XVI

GOING TO CHURCH

"But having entered in, we shall find there
Silence, and sudden dimness, and deep prayer,
And faces of crowned angels all about."

— Rossetti.

Elsie woke on Sunday morning with her thoughts full of the charms of Wayne's Court.

She pictured the place to herself in the silence of the early hours, the cool depths of shadow in the green aisles, the trimly-kept gardens, the first sunshine stealing along the grey terrace. Did Arnold Wayne care for her well enough to ask her to come and reign over his old home?

He liked her, she was sure of that. And his cousins detested her, of that she was sure also. No woman can ever endure the thought that she is disliked or despised by the relatives of the man she loves. And poor Elsie, against her own will, had fallen in love with Arnold Wayne.

Against her own will! And Elsie had always fancied that her will was so strong. She had had several strong likings, and had found out (before it was too late) that a strong liking is only a distant cousin to love. For the first time in her life she was beginning to feel that terrible self-distrust which is love's cruel companion. And it is a painful moment for a woman when she learns that the sound of one voice can set her heart throbbing and drive the colour out of her cheeks.

Mrs. Lennard stoutly affirmed that she was quite equal to walking to church and back again. Nobody should get pony-chaises out for her on a Sunday. So the two old ladies and the younger one came out into the lane, just in time to see the flutter of summer gowns on the meadow-path. The Danforths were ahead of them. Yes; and Mrs. Verdon, slim and cool and graceful in a dainty costume of blue-grey cashmere — a dress which wrung unwilling admiration even from the rector's wife.

"That straw-coloured woman dresses well," she said to Elsie. "What a miracle of self-worship she is!"

"But she has a kind heart," Elsie answered. "Think of her love for Jamie."

The boy, trotting by nurse's side, had gone on in front of Mrs. Verdon and the Danforths. They were moving so slowly along the path that the party from Willow Farm instinctively began to saunter. There was a consciousness among them that it would be best for Miss Kilner and the Danforths not to meet too often.

But if they were sauntering, some one behind them was coming on with rapid strides. Arnold Wayne joined them with a cheery greeting.

"You are early," he said. "Do you keep your clocks too fast at the Farm? Miss Kilner, isn't this pure air delicious after London?"

Mrs. Lennard allowed herself to be displaced, and he stepped close to Elsie's side. It was a sultry morning; but the odour of the grass, fresh with half-hidden streams, was in the air. The meadow was dotted with yellow-rayed flowers, and in the moist places the tall bulrush lifted its dark brown head.

"Yes," Elsie answered, with a sigh of satisfaction; "it makes it hard to think of going back to a 'long, unlovely street.'"

"You are not going back yet," he said quickly. And the earnest look which accompanied the words brought the colour into her face.

"Not yet," she responded; "but one's bright days always fly."

The tone touched his heart. It told him that her bright days had been few. What he would have said was never known; words were rising to his lips when Mary Danforth came running back to them at a girlish speed.

"Oh, Arnold, how you are loitering!" she said, panting. "You will be late at church, naughty boy! It's a dreadful thing for the Squire to set a bad example, Miss Kilner."

"Isn't it rather warm for such violent exercise, Mary?" he asked in a lazy voice. "A cool face is a blessing to its possessor and all beholders."

Mary had the complexion that flushes easily. The glow which overspread her face was not becoming, but she felt that she was a martyr in a good cause. She had run back to separate her cousin from the dangerous Miss Kilner. Lily, whose eyes were on Francis, was hastening after her.

As to Francis, he was beginning to be piqued by Elsie's gentle indifference, and he had a vague suspicion that Wayne was carrying on a flirtation with her instead of attending to Mrs. Verdon. Lily's light-grey eyes were not as beautiful as Elsie's brown orbs, but they were pretty enough when they glanced at him in mute reproach. He felt he had neglected Lily.

Mrs. Verdon did not follow the Danforths when they ran back to the Willow Farm people. She sauntered slowly on talking with their father; but, when the two parties came together and melted into one, her greetings were very gracious.

Elsie, who was somehow edged out of the group, found herself walking alone. The Danforths were breaking the quietness of the meadows with their laughing voices. She was glad to escape them and overtake nurse and Jamie.

The boy met her gladly, putting his little warm hand into hers. And only a woman with a heartache can understand the comfort that she found in the clasp of that childish hand.

"We're going to church," said Jamie. "You shall sit by my side. It ain't a very pretty church."

"Oh, Master Jamie, 'ain't' again!" nurse murmured, in a tone of mild reproof.

"But there's nice things in it," continued Jamie, paying no attention to the good woman. "There's a man, cut out of stone, lying on his back, and he's lost his nose. He twies to put his hands together, but can't, not properly, 'cos some of his fingers has come off."

"I should like to see him," remarked Elsie, "very much."

"I'll show him to you, when the pweachin's done," Jamie promised. "Keep close to me."

She did keep close to him when they entered the little grey church, and found a sense of peace and quietness there. She sat by his side, close to a massive pillar, near an open window set deep in the ancient wall. The breath of the warm summer wandered in, and she did not criticise the singing or the sermon. Through it all she could hear the distant bleating of flocks and the hum of bees.

If she could always live a simple country life with Jamie, it would be full of calm content. But the boy would grow up and demand more than her slender means could provide; and he belonged to Mrs. Verdon. She did not think she could endure a country life without Jamie. It would be better to go back to the London street, and care for the children of the poor, than live in rural solitude.

"Come and see the stone man," whispered Jamie, as soon as the service was over.

She let him lead her into a side aisle where a battered knightly figure lay on an altar-tomb. It was still and cool in this dim nook, and faint lights and shadows fell softly on the old warrior in his repose. The boy stood looking at him in silence.

"I wonder who he was," Elsie said in a low voice.

"His name was Lionel de Wayne," replied Arnold, at her elbow; "and he was one of the goodliest knights that ever bare shield. 'His soul is with the saints, I trust.'"

"Amen," said Elsie gravely. Jamie looked up at both the speakers with big blue eyes.

"I have some records of him at the Court," Arnold went on. "You must come and turn them over some day; if you care about such things, you will find a store."

"I do care," she answered. "Why do you not write a book about the Court, Mr. Wayne? England likes to know the histories of her stately old houses, and there is a great deal to tell."

"We will write it together," he said; and her heart gave a sudden throb.

"We had lost you!" Mary Danforth exclaimed behind the pair. "Arnold, Mrs. Verdon has promised to lunch with us; won't you come too?"

"I'll think about it," he replied, relapsing into that lazy manner which his friends knew so well.

"There isn't much time to think of it," said Mary, rather sharply. "You know father likes his luncheon punctually at half-past one."

"Don't let him wait for me. I was always a dawdling fellow."

Jamie held Elsie's hand as they walked home through the meadows. Miss Ryan asked Mrs. Verdon to let her keep him at Willow Farm for the rest of the day, and Elsie spent the long afternoon hours with the boy.

Seeing that Francis Ryan was prowling about in the garden, she carried Jamie off to her large, cool room upstairs, and told him stories to his heart's content. Then, too, she had discovered a pile of nursery books in a corner of the house, and had brought them up here for his benefit. Their hearts grew closer and closer together; they enjoyed each other's love, and exchanged caresses like a couple of children. The child had a wonderfully freshening influence on Elsie's life, and when she brought him down to afternoon tea, the two old ladies rejoiced to see her looking so young and bright.

"Francis is gone to the Danforths'," said Mrs. Lennard, with a merry twinkle in her eyes.

The afternoon was deepening into evening when Arnold Wayne came up the garden path to the door. He found Elsie under the porch, with a mass of jessamine hanging over her head.

"There is to be a picnic next Thursday," he said; "I am dragged into it. The gathering-place will be in a meadow, under some trees near the river. I've got a little boat, and a man to row people to and from the island."

"I shall like that," remarked Jamie, who was listening. "Mammy will be sure to let me go!"

Elsie did not feel strongly inclined to go to the picnic. She had taken the quiet of the country into her heart, and wanted to escape from society. But Mrs. Lennard disapproved of this growing taste for solitude.

"You must mingle with the others, my dear, whether you like them or not," she said. "I shall come upstairs and turn over your dresses. You have a cool, brown holland-looking thing, trimmed with bands of scarlet silk and black lace. I think you shall wear that."

CHAPTER XVII

THE PICNIC

> "The chatterers chatter, here and there,
> They chatter of they know not what."
>
> —Owen Meredith.

"The cool, brown holland-looking thing" was donned, in obedience to Mrs. Lennard's decree. Mrs. Verdon had written to her milliner to send her down something new for the occasion in the shape of headgear. But Elsie had spent an hour in her room, on the day before the picnic, and had retrimmed a black chip hat with black lace and soft knots of scarlet ribbon.

"I am not a rich woman," she said to the rector's wife; "and if I were, I should still like to use the gifts that have been given me. I think we should not let any gift get rusty for lack of use."

"You would have made an excellent wife for a poor man, my dear," Mrs. Lennard remarked.

"I shall never be any man's wife," said Elsie. "I mean to be a little sister of the poor, and especially devote myself to children. That is my vocation; I see it plainly."

"Indeed"—Mrs. Lennard leaned back in her chair with a satisfied little smile as she surveyed her favourite—"I don't think I would adopt that kind of dress just yet, if I were you. Black lace and a touch of scarlet are very becoming."

The day of the picnic was as balmy and blue as those that had gone before. The dew was still hanging on the clustered white roses which climbed to her latticed casement when Elsie looked out. The sweet, wet blossoms touched her face as she leaned forward into the pure morning air.

Her window overlooked that side of the garden nearest to the lane; and some one, strolling between the leafy hedges, looked up and saw a vision of a bright yet delicate face, framed in a quantity of thick, dark, rumpled hair.

He stood still, well hidden by the screen of leaves, and gazed upward in silent delight. The pretty picture only lasted half a minute; she vanished, and he, finding that the casement remained a blank, went back over a gate, and across dew-wet fields, to his solitary breakfast.

The picnic was exactly like other picnics. A space of level turf, under the shade of some fine beeches, had been chosen as the banqueting-place.

It was quite an aristocratic gathering; most of the important people of the country were there. There were white and rose-colour, violet and primrose, showing out amongst other indescribable tints. Frilled parasols were unfurled like great flowers; the place was filled with dainty fabrics, and soft hues, and laughter and ceaseless movement. All this flutter and commotion made Elsie feel intensely quiet. Somehow, although she was by no means unnoticed, she could not enter into the spirit of the hour.

Jamie did not care about the ladies and their pretty dresses; but he appreciated the good things to eat. Mrs. Verdon had said that he was too young to be of the party, but had ended by bringing him. Home was only a little way off, and nurse was among the other servants. Meanwhile the boy had stationed himself by Elsie's side, and she was keeping a careful watch over his plate.

Arnold saw them sitting together on the edge of the crowd, and longed to join them. But the party had assembled in his field, and he had a host's duties to perform. His father's friends came round him, glad to see that he had returned to the Court; elderly men proffered advice about this matter and that, taking it for granted that he would be a wanderer no more; matrons regarded him with motherly eyes. And Elsie silently thought that he looked like a prince upon his own borders, bidding them all welcome.

Lily Danforth, with two girl friends from the other side of the county, was sitting near her. The men moved about helping everybody, supplying their own needs in a rambling fashion. It was altogether a gay, informal kind of affair.

"I suppose it must be true," one of the girls said. "It was Henry who told us the news. He said that her horses bolted, and Mr. Wayne stopped them, and then it turned out that they had heard of each other for years. Such a story can have but one ending."

"I think the ending is pretty certain," Lily answered with gay confidence. "In fact, he has confessed as much to my father. We are all delighted. She is charming; and we were afraid he would settle down as a confirmed bachelor, or not settle at all."

"She is really pretty, and so distinguished looking," the other girl joined in. "I hope she'll give no end of balls at the Court. Just look at her now!"

Involuntarily following the direction of the speaker's glance, Elsie saw Mrs. Verdon and Arnold. He was putting something into her plate, and she was gazing up at him with eyes that seemed no longer wanting in colour and expression. Whether he returned that gaze or not, Elsie, at the moment, could not tell. But, being a woman in love, she jumped to the conclusion that he did.

Moreover, there were Lily's words to ring in her ears like a chime: "In fact, he has confessed as much to my father."

A sudden heart-sinking made her inexpressibly weary of her surroundings, and then she rallied, angry with herself — rallied just in time to see Jamie taking a second plateful of cherry-tart.

"Not a bit more, little man," she said resolutely. "Everybody else has finished. You wouldn't like to sit here and eat all alone. I think we had better get up and come away from the dishes."

"I want to go in the boat; Mr. Wayne said I might."

Jamie really felt that he had had enough, and the boat at this moment was better than the tart.

"Well, dear, you shall go. We'll walk down to the river-side."

There was an island on the river, which was, as Arnold had said, a wonderful place for wild-flowers. It was a very small islet, overgrown with bush vegetation; willow-boughs drooped down into the water; rushes, sedges, and wild trailing things flourished in uncontrolled luxuriance. Sometimes men and boys landed on it when they went fishing in a leaky old boat, or pulled round it to get water-lilies; but it was rumoured that Mr. Wayne would make improvements there.

Already, instead of the old boat, there was a new one, dark green with a stripe of white, moored against the landing-stage at the end of the meadow; and old Giles, who had worked on the Wayne estate for years, was waiting to take anybody for a row.

Miss Kilner and Jamie were the first to come to the river-side. The other people were still lingering over the remains of the feast, making plans, proposing excursions, or chatting about nothing. Jamie had already made the old man's acquaintance, and hailed him as a friend.

"Now carefully, young master. Sit steady," said Giles, as he put his passengers in the stern.

The water under the banks was dark with shadows, but they floated out of the shade into a strange stillness and glory. The voices and laughter in the meadow grew fainter and fainter; they were going away from the turmoil into a world of peace.

Jamie sat still, resting one dimpled hand on Elsie's knee, enjoying it all in silence. It was a calm, full river, running still and smooth even out in the middle current, but the sun shone down, and the oars struck out diamonds.

Giles pulled close to the island, where there was a landing-place, rotten and green with slippery water-weeds. Jamie asked to land and search for the eggs of water-fowl; but Elsie reminded him that other people would be wanting the boat.

As they rowed back again, Giles described the habits of the birds which frequented this reedy spot. Jamie listened open-eyed to his accounts of the moor-hen, flapper, coot, water-rail, dab-chick, and sand-piper, to say nothing of rats in abundance, and an otter now and then. If you crept upon the islet very quietly, you could hear the rats before you saw them. Carefully listening to the sounds, you frequently discovered the rat himself, generally on the stump of some old tree, or on the bare part of the bank overhanging the water. There he would be, sitting upon his hind-legs, holding in his fore-feet the root of a bulrush, and champing away with his sharp teeth so as to be heard at a considerable distance.

"They be a bad lot, the rats—a bad, destructive lot," said the old man solemnly. "I wonder why such vermin was made. You'd never believe the number of fish and young wild-ducks, and game of different sorts, which are eaten up every season by them slippery rascals."

CHAPTER XVIII

THE ISLAND

> "What hath life been? What will it be?
> How have I lived without thee? How
> Is life both lost and found in thee?
> Feel'st thou For ever in this Now?"
>
> —Owen Meredith.

People were coming down to the river when the boat touched the bank again; there was a large group gathered at the landing-place. Two men started forward to help Miss Kilner to step on shore.

Elsie's good angel must surely have taken wing at that moment. With a bright smile, and a sudden flashing look from her dark eyes, she gave her hand to Francis Ryan, and then, chancing to make a false step, she nearly fell into his arms.

He was charmed, puzzled, delighted. Brown eyes sometimes say more than they mean, and Elsie never knew how much seemed to be conveyed in that flashing look. Had she awakened all at once to the knowledge that Francis (with a very little encouragement) was willing to lay himself and all his worldly goods at her feet?

Arnold Wayne was puzzled too, and a sharp pain smote him to the heart.

Was this the woman who had spoken to him in the little London room, with a voice like that of an angel? Then they had seemed to stand on the threshold of a beautiful life to be. There had been the unuttered consciousness of a comfort that each could give—a feeling of need and longing that each could fill.

And that golden hour had gone by. She was only a flirt, after all; more clever and more refined than the other flirts he had known, but just as unreal and unscrupulous as the rest.

She did not know what she had done. It seems to be a long way down from the mountain-top to the common earth at its base; but a woman can accomplish the descent in a moment.

She was very beautiful, certainly; he had not discovered until this instant what a power of witchery lurked in those dark eyes. He had gazed into their brown depths as a man who looks deep into a crystal pool, thinking that he sees all that is there.

She had not looked at him when she rejected his aid and sprang out with the help of Francis. She did not look at him when she turned and took Jamie by the hand.

"Are you not tired of the boy yet?" asked Mrs. Verdon's silvery voice. "You are very kind, dear Miss Kilner; but pray send him to nurse if he wearies you."

"He does not weary me in the least," Elsie answered, looking smilingly into Katherine's face. She could smile unflinchingly, although she saw that Arnold was staying by the "fair ladye's" side.

"Let them go their way together," she thought. "After all, what right have I to care?"

As to Francis Ryan, he forgot that Lily Danforth was looking after him with glances full of the deepest reproach. He had never been thoroughly in love with Lily; he had only felt for her that spurious kind of love which grows out of proximity. But she, poor girl, had set all her hopes upon him, and was very miserable when she saw what Elsie had done. She began to think that she had made an enemy of Miss Kilner.

"It was Mary's fault," she thought bitterly. "Mary decided that we should give her the cold shoulder. 'We don't know who she is,' she said. Absurd! It would have been better to have been civil."

Elsie, too, had forgotten Lily. The hint which Arnold had given her about the old attachment between his cousin and Ryan had slipped out of her mind. She was intent on wearing a brave face before the world, and hiding all the outward and visible signs of heartache.

Yet there was no need to hide a pain which no one suspected her of enduring. No one, save Mrs. Lennard, had discovered that Elsie had a secret, and the old lady could keep her own counsel.

"I have scarcely had a word from you all day," said Francis, not caring to conceal his delight as he walked up the meadow by her side.

"I did not know that my words were of any value," Elsie answered.

The flush was still warm on her cheek, and the dangerous light still shone in her eyes. Under the shade of her black lace hat the face glowed like a rich flower.

"Is that quite true, Miss Kilner?" asked Francis, looking down at her with undisguised admiration. "I think you must know that any word of yours—even the lightest—is of value to me."

"I'm afraid I say a great many foolish words," she replied lightly. "And they are best forgotten. What a glorious day we are having! This is Jamie's first picnic, and he will look back on it in years to come as a joy for ever. Rushbrook is certainly a charming place."

"Could you be content to live in Rushbrook?" Ryan suddenly asked.

"Always? I don't know."

"Try and see if you get tired of it, Miss Kilner."

"I am not tired of it yet," she said hurriedly, half afraid that he would go too far. "It is a place to remember and dream of on a November day in London."

"Do you realise that we are not very far from November?" Francis said. "We are only divided from that dreaded month by September and October. And they will go by like a dream; they always do. 'Gather ye rosebuds while ye may.'"

"I've been gathering them ever since I came here, Mr. Ryan. Don't talk of November now; I hate it."

"I should not hate it," he murmured, "if we could spend it together."

"Here is Mrs. Lennard looking for me," exclaimed Elsie hastily. "I have lost sight of her too long."

She went quickly towards her old friend, who received her with questioning eyes.

"You are getting too warm, my dear," Mrs. Lennard said. "Come and sit down in a cool spot. Mrs. Appleby has been wanting to chat with you; she knew your mother years ago."

Elsie found Mrs. Appleby on a camp-stool under the beeches, and sank down on the grass by her side. Mrs. Lennard took possession of Jamie, and kept him quiet by telling him an enchanting story.

The talk about old days soothed Elsie, and brought her, unawares, into a better state of mind. Mrs. Appleby knew nothing of the storm that she was helping to still. She chatted on, pleasantly and calmly, about those who had done with all storms for ever and ever; and by-and-by the young woman beside her began to remember that the struggle is short, and the rest long.

They were drinking tea under the trees when the wanderers came dropping in, by twos and threes, from all points of the compass. Among the latest were Arnold and Mrs. Verdon—a goodly pair.

People smiled furtively, and exchanged meaning glances when these two arrived. Arnold's eyes sought for the person who still interested him above all others, in spite of the shock she had given him. His heart was comforted when he saw her sitting quietly under a gigantic beech by an old lady's side.

"Dear Elsie," Jamie whispered, "I've had enough tea. It'll soon be my bedtime. Take me down to the boat and let me have just one row more, and then give me to nurse."

At the same moment Mrs. Lennard was addressing Francis in her most persuasive voice.

"Dear Mr. Ryan, you are doing nothing, and we are all so comfortably idle here in the shade. It will be most kind if you will hold my skein of yarn."

The young man held out his hands with ready obedience. Elsie was only two or three yards away, and he was content.

A few moments later Miss Kilner rose and took Jamie by the hand; and at the same instant Mrs. Verdon gave a sudden exclamation.

"I have left my little white shawl in the boat!" she cried. "It's a dear little shawl. I wouldn't lose it for the world."

"I will get it for you," Elsie said readily. "Jamie and I are going down to the boat before he says 'Good-night.'"

"Oh, thanks!" Mrs. Verdon responded gratefully; and then she glanced at Arnold, as if she expected him to sit down beside her on the grass.

But he remained standing bolt upright for a second. Then he took a stride in Elsie's direction. "I think I'll look after the shawl myself," he was heard to say. "Giles's old brain is apt to get confused after any kind of excitement."

Francis Ryan made an uneasy movement, but he was tied and bound with the skein of yarn; and Mrs. Lennard, winding steadily, was smiling into his eyes.

The hand which held Jamie unconsciously tightened its grasp, and the boy looked up in surprise.

"Why do you squeeze me so hard, Elsie?" he asked. "I ain't going to run away."

She did not reply; her heart was throbbing fast, and Arnold found that even the most commonplace remark stuck in his throat somehow. They walked for some yards together in silence.

"I hope you have had a pleasant day," he said at last.

"Very pleasant," she answered; "and Jamie has been the best of good boys."

"Yes, I've been very good indeed," remarked that gentleman in a tone of self-congratulation. "And I didn't eat too much, did I?"

"Well, there was the cherry tart; I had to take away your second plateful."

Arnold laughed, and the laugh seemed to set them at ease again.

They walked on quickly over the starry yellow flowers in the grass. The bright day would have a golden ending; already there were amber lights shining calmly on the river.

Giles, half asleep at the landing-stage, looked up as they approached, and drew the back of his hand across his tired old eyes. Arnold seemed to be moved by a sudden impulse.

"There's a white shawl left in the boat," he said. "Take it back to Mrs. Verdon, Giles, at once. You'll find her somewhere under the beeches. Now, Jamie, I'll pull across to the island myself. Step in, Miss Kilner."

It did not occur to Elsie to disobey him. A minute after, when they were floating out upon the water, she thought that she had been too submissive. But he was pulling away with long, steady strokes, right away into the middle of the golden light.

There was very little said just then. They glided on in a delicious stillness; and presently the boat ran close to some old worn steps that were half hidden by tall, coarse grass, and was made fast. Arnold had determined to land on the island.

"Come," he said, almost imperiously.

"I didn't think of this," Elsie answered, her colour coming and going, "and we shall be missed. It is time for Jamie to go home."

"No, it isn't," said Jamie gaily, as Arnold lifted him out upon the decayed little pier.

A path led from the pier through a thicket of wild foliage, and then they came to a clear space and a little thatched hut shaped like a bee-hive. There was nothing in it save an old pair of oars and a broken basket, but the place had been kept in pretty good repair.

Right in front of the hut the underwood had been cleared away, and the ground sloped gently down to the water. The slow, full, golden river was flowing on, and they stood silently watching the tide.

"We are out of the world here," Arnold said at last. "One could fancy that Father Time sometimes comes to this forgotten island and sits down to rest. Nothing has changed here since I was a boy; the trees have grown thicker and taller, that is all."

"Somebody said that you were going to improve the island," Elsie remarked. "I hardly see how that can be done."

"I merely thought of making it more habitable," he replied. "It would be possible to establish Giles and his wife very comfortably here. They are living now in a disreputable old cottage which ought to have been pulled down years ago."

"Then you think of building a nice little house instead of that bee-hive hut?"

"Yes; the house can be made as picturesque as the hut, you know. One can look forward to pleasant parties here—children's picnics, and that kind of thing."

Elsie thought she knew what he was thinking of at that moment. He was going to settle down at the Court with Katherine, and she would play the part of Lady Bountiful to perfection; children's picnics were quite in her line, and perhaps she had already suggested that the island was the very spot for such gatherings. It was all right, of course; every one would say that he had chosen wisely. But, as he had chosen, why was he standing here with another woman by his side?

"Let us go now," she said suddenly, conscious of an unnatural tone in her voice. "The light is fading; it is time to join the others."

He looked at her, but she was still watching the flow of the river, and did not meet his eyes.

"Is there any need for such haste?" he asked. "I haven't said many words to you to-day. Old friends have been crowding round me, and — — "

"Naturally," she broke in coldly; "but you can talk as well anywhere else. And Jamie must be sent to bed."

She turned sharply away towards the path by which they had come to the clearing. Then all at once she spoke in another tone —

"What has become of the child?"

"He was standing close to you a moment ago," Arnold answered quickly. "Jamie, where are you? Jamie!" he called, in a loud, ringing voice.

Elsie went flying along the path with the speed of some hunted wild creature. All else was forgotten in her intense anxiety. She had been absorbed in her own foolish feelings, she thought bitterly, and had left the boy to his own devices. How wrong it was to have lost sight of him for an instant in such a perilous spot! Oh that she had never brought him here!

She seemed to have suffered hours of misery in those few seconds of suspense. The path turned abruptly, opening out upon the little pier, and just at the turn she was confronted by Jamie himself. He met her with a very red face.

"I done it," he began confusedly. "No, I never done it exactly, but it's gone. It come untied. I gived it one tug, and I nearly tumbled in."

"Oh, you naughty boy, to go close to the edge of the water!" sobbed Elsie, catching him in her arms and kissing him. "I won't let you leave me for an instant till I put you into nurse's hands. My own dear, troublesome darling! If anything had happened to you I should have died!" She was not conscious of Arnold's presence just then. Words poured fast from her lips as she held the boy to her heart in an ecstasy of relief. She was still on her knees upon the path, still trembling like a leaf, when Mr. Wayne's voice fell upon her ear.

"Well, of all the young rascals I ever met, he's the biggest! Why, you scamp, what made you do such a thing?"

"I never done it exactly. I—I—just gived it one tug. I—I——" Jamie's quivering lips failed to complete the sentence. His face worked like a queer gutta-percha visage for a moment, and then he burst into a hearty roar which must have startled every living thing on the island.

Arnold muttered something which was luckily drowned by Jamie's noise. The boat was gone; the burning glory of sunset was slowly dying out, and across the river came the first faint breath of the night. He was here on a desolate island, with a woman who did not care for him, and he had cared for her so much that his love was the very crown of his life. Her indifference would not make any outward change in him. He was not the kind of man to believe that his heart was broken, but he knew that he should feel the want of her as long as he lived; he felt that he might have risen to a higher level if she had put her hand in his and walked by his side. At first he had not for a moment doubted that she could be won. He had believed that she was meant for him; he had triumphed in anticipation, but some nameless barrier had risen between them and baffled him, and now it was all over. If the boat had not got loose and drifted away, he would have rowed her back in a sullen silence which would never have been broken again.

But there was no boat, and Elsie, still crooning over Jamie, did not yet understand what had happened. When the boy had ceased bellowing for very weariness, she suggested that they should all go home as quickly as they could. The child had been over-excited and over-tired with his long day.

"It is not wise to kneel on the damp earth," said Arnold, with cold tranquillity. "Let me advise you to get up and take Jamie into the hut. The dew is beginning to fall."

"Into the hut?" repeated Elsie, rising from her knees and turning her pale face towards him.

"Yes. The boat is gone."

"Gone! Then how shall we go back? What can we do?"

"I must think." His voice was still very quiet. "You had better take him into the hut."

She obeyed in silence, half stupefied and bewildered after the agitation she had undergone. The boy had sobbed himself into a drowsy state, and staggered along the path supported by her arm. When they entered the hut she laid him on the seat, and made a pillow of the old basket, covered with her handkerchief. In a moment he was fast asleep.

When she came out of the little building Arnold was standing in the clearing, looking out across the water. The last of the sunset had vanished, and the river and its banks looked like a picture in delicate grey tints. A light suddenly twinkled on the opposite shore, where one could just discern the outlines of a farm-house, fading fast into the mist of twilight.

"Can we not make a signal?" Elsie asked.

"We can gather sticks and light a fire," he answered gravely. "There's nothing else to be done."

"There's plenty of wood," she said, "and you have some matches, I suppose? I'll help you to collect the boughs and twigs." She made a movement towards the underwood, but he stopped her, and their hands touched.

"You are cold," he said, "and you had a great fright. I wish I could have prevented all this."

"I think," she replied, "that it is quite as unpleasant for you as for me."

"Not half as unpleasant," he returned abruptly. "You must hate me for bringing you here. You do hate me, don't you?"

He was holding the little cold hand in his and chafing it gently.

"No," she answered, pulling her hand away; "but we are wasting time. Mrs. Lennard will be anxious about me, and— —"

"And what?"

She faltered; her voice fell and broke. Then she looked up proudly, and her eyes met his with a defiant glance.

"And Mrs. Verdon will be inconsolable without you."

When she had spoken she turned from him and began breaking off the boughs which hung low enough for her to reach. He looked down at her slender, graceful figure, and a great tremor passed over him. The next instant she felt him close at her side.

"You must not do that," he said. "Elsie, listen! Some one has been telling falsehoods. Mrs. Verdon is nothing more to me than a pleasant acquaintance. I am grateful to her for taking care of Jamie; but you know I always feel that Waring meant to leave the boy to me. Perhaps I was wrong to bring you here; I wanted a few quiet words—I wanted to get you all to myself for five minutes."

She did not speak, and her head was drooping. The bough that she had held was released, and sprang back, rustling its foliage. The stillness, the grey light, the heavy shadows of the trees, gave a strange unreality to the moment. She felt as if she were part of some bewildering dream.

"I have thought of you every hour of the day," he went on. "I have been thinking of you ever since I saw you first. When we talked together in your London room, I hoped that you were beginning to be interested in me."

She stirred a little, and then lifted her face. She looked as he remembered her looking when he had first known her, only that she was very pale now.

"I was—interested," she said.

All the ordinary conventional barriers had fallen away between them. He found himself face to face with the beloved woman he had fancied lost for ever.

"Elsie," he whispered, "Elsie, won't you try to care for me? Won't you come to me and help me to live my life in the right way? I want a wife's help and a wife's love. Elsie, come!"

She made a slight movement towards him. His arms were round her in an instant, his warm lips pressed to hers; and in the supreme felicity of that moment, time, place, circumstances, were all forgotten. They had passed together into that earthly paradise whose gates are still opened to some favoured mortals in this vale of tears.

"Hilloo! Hilloo!"

It was old Giles's voice, hoarse as a raven's; and although it startled them rudely, it was a welcome sound. Elsie went into the hut to rouse Jamie as gently as she could, and Arnold listened to Giles's explanation of his arrival.

He had been at the landing-stage waiting for his master's return, when a couple of lads came rowing in with the empty boat. They were fishing on the river, and had found it adrift and captured it. So Giles, guessing what had happened, had pulled off to the island without a moment's delay.

Jamie, a little cross and very sleepy, was taken home to his bed at The Cedars in a half-awake condition; and afterwards Elsie and Arnold strolled along Miss Ryan's garden in the gloaming, the happiest pair of lovers that ever saw the moon rise over Rushbrook in silent peace.

"Something told me that the day would have a good ending," said Mrs. Lennard, as she wished Elsie good-night.

CHAPTER XIX

CONCLUSION

> "And now those vivid hours are gone,
> Like mine own life to me thou art.
> Where past and present, wound in one,
> Do make a garland for the heart."
>
> — Tennyson.

It was the evening of the day after the picnic, and all Rushbrook had already heard the news. The Danforths had heard it in the morning from Arnold himself, and Mrs. Verdon had heard it in the afternoon from the Danforths.

Katherine Verdon was an unemotional woman. She did not feel in the least inclined to go into hysterics or make bitter speeches. Mrs. Tell, who watched her narrowly, could not detect the slightest change in her demeanour. She remarked that Miss Kilner was very pretty—really quite beautiful—and no one could be surprised at the turn that things had taken.

"I don't know," replied her sister-in-law; "I confess I am surprised. He ought to have married somebody in a better position."

"Oh, her position is good enough," Mrs. Verdon answered, "and she will suit him exactly. He is a man who will demand a great deal of devotion from his wife, and she will give him all he needs. It would have been bad for him if he had married a woman whose supply was not equal to the demand."

"What do you suppose would have happened in that case?" Mrs. Tell asked.

"She would have been bored, and he would have been disappointed and restless. I think he would have taken to wandering again; but there is no fear of that now. You will see that this will be an ideal marriage."

Having said this, Katherine went quietly out of the room and took her way upstairs to the side of Jamie's bed. He was asleep; but the heat had flushed him, and he tossed the bed-clothes away from his rosy limbs and murmured in his sleep. Nurse had gone down to her supper; there was no one to see Katherine as she bent over the child with a look of tenderness in her eyes.

"My life is in my own hands," she thought.

"I have not given up myself to any one else, and it is better as it is. I love the boy; he is the only thing I really care for."

Just then he gave another toss, and opened his eyes with a fretful little wail. Seeing Katharine, he put out his arms and said, "Mammy!"

She soothed him with her sweet voice and soft touch, gave him a draught of lemonade, and then laid him down again, calmed and refreshed, to fall into a deep slumber. Yes, it was all well, she repeated to herself; she had her own life, her own pleasures, her own ways; to give up anything that was hers, to change any of her plans, would have cost her more than it costs most women. She was not fond of making sacrifices; she had never loved well enough to know the sweetness of self-surrender.

Arnold Wayne had taken her fancy, but he had never won her heart. It is true that he had not tried to win it, and Katherine did not care to ask herself whether he would have succeeded if he had tried. She had felt one slight pang of jealousy when she had been told of his engagement, and that was all. This quiet half-hour spent by Jamie's bed had set everything right in her life. She understood herself now, and could even think of something pretty to give Miss Kilner for a wedding present.

"Jamie shall give her something from himself," she decided. "He is very fond of her, and she is really a nice woman. I wish them well—yes, in all sincerity I wish them well."

If there were others who did not feel as kindly as Katherine did, there was no manifestation of ill-will. The Danforths had expected Mrs. Verdon to join them in bewailing the foolish match, but she had quietly and cleverly disappointed them. They had left her with the impression that they must have been mistaken in her from the first. She had never thought as seriously of Arnold as they had supposed; she had amused herself with their schemes and hopes, and that was all.

"I was never sure of her from the beginning," said Mr. Danforth to his daughters. "She has been always perfectly contented with her position. There were no signs of restlessness about her at all. But you girls are dead sure of everything; when you take a notion into your heads you can't listen to reason."

He had been very cross all day, finding fault with everything that "the girls" said and did, until he had driven them both to the verge of desperation; and Lily, when she went upstairs to dress for dinner, was wondering how she should get through that miserable meal without bursting into a great fit of crying.

She thought how happy Elsie Kilner must be at that moment with Arnold as her declared lover. No doubt Francis Ryan was moping about Willow Farm in a state of unacknowledged wretchedness. She was sure that Francis had really liked that girl; she had seen his feelings plainly on the day of the picnic. Perhaps he would go away altogether from Rushbrook, unable to bear the sight of his rival's happiness. And this was to be the ending of Lily's dream!

But it is best not to be too certain about endings and beginnings; they look so like each other sometimes, and are apt to be so oddly mixed up in our lives.

When you are thoroughly heart-sick and hopeless, dress is quite an unimportant thing. Lily put on a cream-white cashmere gown which had seen its best days, noticed that the skirt was soiled, and said with Mr. Toots that it was of no consequence. There were some clusters of pink geranium in a glass on her table, and she pinned them on her bodice in a dejected fashion. Then she went downstairs slowly, with her bright cheeks paler than usual and all her sprightliness gone.

The lights were golden on the lawn, and the great cedar was casting velvety shadows there. Her father was standing under the old tree, looking so jovial and radiant that she marvelled at the sudden change in his mood. Some one, who stood with his back towards the house, was in close conversation with Mr. Danforth.

"Here she is, Ryan!" her father said, as he saw her through the open door. "Here she is! Let her come out and answer for herself."

Francis Ryan turned, and Lily, shy and trembling, went out in obedience to Mr. Danforth's call. Perhaps her hesitation and timidity became her better than self-confidence; anyhow, Francis thought that he had never seen her look so pretty as she did at this moment, when she came bashfully towards him under the old cedar with a pensive look on her young face.

"He has come to ask me for you, Lily," said Mr. Danforth, glowing with satisfaction. "He has my consent, and now you must give him your answer."

Then the head of the family went off to find Mary and tell her the joyful news, and Francis and Lily stood under the dark cedar-boughs together hand in hand. She was too happy to know exactly what he was saying; she only knew that she had managed to say what was required of her, and that life had suddenly changed from gloom to glory.

September had set in, and only a few stragglers had come back to London. Most people were still lingering on the sea-shore or among the breezy hills; but one young woman, standing at the window of a back-room in All Saints' Street, was looking as happy as if she loved the view of chimney-pots and smoky tiles.

It was the last day of Elsie's single life. The bell was just beginning to chime for five o'clock service; in the next room Mrs. Lennard and Miss Saxon were closing the lids of the boxes and looking round to see that nothing had been forgotten or left out. And Elsie, standing alone in her old place, was watching the sunset shining on these crowded house-roofs for the last time. Meta's manuscript, carefully tied up, was lying on the little table near. As Elsie's fingers rested on the roll, her thoughts went straying back to that evening in the early spring when she had stood here to fight her battle in silence.

It was not until that battle had been fought and won that she had known the guidance of the vanished hand; and now, in the golden quietness of this hour, she recalled some lines from "In Memoriam" which seemed to come with new freshness of meaning to her mind: —

> "In vain shalt thou, or any, call
> The spirits from their golden day,
> Except, like them, thou too canst say,
> My spirit is at peace with all."

Robert and Bertha were forgiven, although the old home had passed into the hands of strangers, and the old haunts would know her footsteps no more. Mr. Lennard, too, had given up the living in Sussex, and would come, later on, to settle in Rushbrook, near Wayne's Court. Mrs. Lennard had declared that it was impossible for her to live far away from her adopted daughter, and Elsie longed to have this faithful friend always by her side. And Miss Saxon, also, had promised to say good-bye to London, and follow Elsie into her quiet world of meadows and streams. Another summer would bring Mrs. Beaton and her son into that pastoral country, just to refresh themselves with a glimpse of its sweetness and light. How Elsie would welcome the sight of those friendly faces which had gladdened her lonesome days!

To-night for musings; to-morrow for the beginning of the new life. To-night for memories; to-morrow for the clasp of wedded hands and the solemn troth, plighted "till death do us part."

"But there will never be a parting," said Elsie, taking a last look at the fading light of the sunset. "Did not Harold and Meta walk together to the very brink of the river? and is not the vanished hand still pointing to the home of rest upon the other side?"